Out of the Mirrored Garden

NEW FICTION

BY

LATIN AMERICAN

WOMEN

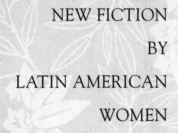

Anchor Books

DOUBLEDAY

NEW YORK
LONDON
TORONTO
SYDNEY
AUCKLAND

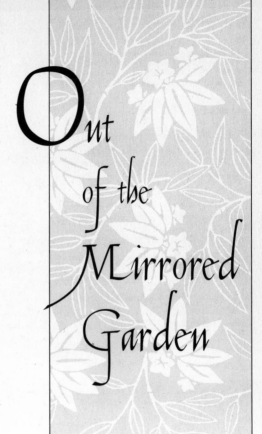

Out of the Mirrored Garden

EDITED BY

Delia Poey

AN ANCHOR BOOK
PUBLISHED BY DOUBLEDAY
a division of Bantam Doubleday Dell Publishing
Group, Inc.
1540 Broadway, New York, New York 10036

ANCHOR BOOKS, DOUBLEDAY, and the portrayal
of an anchor are trademarks of Doubleday, a
division of Bantam Doubleday Dell Publishing
Group, Inc.

Acknowledgments for individual stories appear on
pages 219–22.

Book design by Jennifer Ann Daddio

Library of Congress
Cataloging-in-Publication Data
Out of the mirrored garden : new fiction by Latin
    American women / edited by Delia Poey.
        p.   cm.
        Includes bibliographical references
    (pp. 215–17).
        1. Short stories, Spanish American—
    Translations in English.   2. Spanish American
    fiction—20th century—Translations into
    English.   3. Spanish American fiction—
    Women authors—Translations into English.
    I. Poey, Delia.
    PQ7087.E508   1996
    863—dc20   95-16371
                                            CIP

ISBN 0-385-47594-2
Copyright © 1996 by Delia Poey
Printed in the United States of America
First Anchor Books Edition: January 1996
10   9   8   7   6   5   4   3   2   1

For

Alexandria

&

Gabriela

Editor's Acknowledgments

This anthology is a combined effort, and its publication depended upon the help and encouragement of so many individuals, it would be impossible to list them all. My deepest thanks go to: Elaine Markson of the Elaine Markson Literary Agency for placing the book in the able hands of Arabella Meyer at Anchor Books; to Arabella Meyer for her patience, her willingness to keep an open mind, and her keen eye in the difficult task of editing translations; to Mercedes Barquet of the Colegio de Mexico for helping me contact several writers; to Carmen Esteves and Lizabeth Paravisini-Gebert for their help in contacting Caribbean authors; to Carmen Boullosa for directing me to the fabulous work of Vlady Kociancich and Diamela Eltit; to Susan Bergholtz of the Susan Bergholtz Literary Agency for her help in including the work of Rosario Ferré; to Laura Dail for providing me with the work of Cristina Peri Rossi and Martha Cerda; to Ilan Stavans for bringing the work of Alcina Lubitch Domecq to my attention; to Leslie Bary for her encouragement and advice when the book was just in the "idea stage"; to all of the writers and translators who gave so generously of their time, particularly Julieta Campos and Barbara Jacobs, whom I had the pleasure of meeting in the early stages of the project; to Federico Poey for access to his fax machine and editing my faltering formal Spanish; to Delia Alcazar Poey and Roberto Poey for their frequent visits to bookstores in Mexico City; to my two daughters, Alexandria and Gabriela, for understanding, in their own way, that a closed door means "do not disturb"; and especially to my husband, Virgil Suarez, without whose encouragement, love, and support, not to mention excellent cooking skills, I could never have completed this project.

Contents

Introduction

The title of this anthology, *Out of the Mirrored Garden*, is purposely open to the reader's interpretation. The image of the "mirrored garden" plays on the frequent appearance of labyrinths and mirrors as metaphoric representations of reality in Latin American writing. The image of the garden is one that is particularly pervasive in writing by and about women. The implication that these seventeen stories come *out of* the mirrored garden is also deliberately ambiguous, and can be taken to mean that the works have left behind the mirrored garden, that is, lie outside of the usual assumptions regarding women's fiction and Latin American literature. Or it can be taken to have the opposite meaning —that the works come from within the mirrored garden and are taken out to be presented to the reader. Either interpretation is equally correct since the writers gathered in this collection have a broad array of influences from which to choose, and from which to depart. Some are heirs to the tradition exemplified by writers such as Jorge Luis Borges, Gabriel García Márquez, Carlos Fuentes, and Mario Vargas-Llosa, whose work seemed to explode onto the international literary scene in the sixties, and fittingly earned the label of the "Boom." Others take their writing along different paths.

What these stories all have in common is the fact that they were born of the imaginations, and crafted in the minds, of Latin American women, and as such, share a sense of urgency. As the critic and writer Helena Araujo has pointed out, the Latin American woman writer is in a similar position to that of Scheherazade, the fictional narrator of the *Thousand and One Arabian Nights*. For Scheherazade, spinning tales was a matter of survival. In many ways this is also true of Latin American women writers, for without their tales, a kind of death would result. A death in terms of having to be content with their identity being written by someone else, having their voices silenced, and having their place in history erased.

It was the imminent danger of such a death that drove Sor Juana Inés de la Cruz (1651–95), the brilliant dramatist, essayist, and poet, to choose the convent over marriage, as a place from which she could study and write. Her cell, filled with books, provided her with the time and space necessary for that important task. As Virginia Woolf pointed out three centuries later, a writer needs a "room of her own"; marriage and family rarely provide such luxuries.

Sor Juana Inés de la Cruz's writing often dealt with issues that are still central to Latin American women's literature. She argued eloquently for women's rights, especially the right to literacy and education. In her time and well into the nineteenth century, this position was considered radical, since it was commonly believed that women not only had no use for an education, but that it could actually prove damaging to their moral character. Even the relatively small number of upper-class women who could read and write were heavily censured and dissuaded from pursuing writing in any public sphere. Those who dared to publish their writing had to contend with dire consequences ranging from societal disapproval, excommunication, and forced exile, to complete obliteration, as was the case with Mercedes Cabello de Carbonara (1845–1909) who wrote and published romances, a genre popular with both male and female Latin American authors in the nineteenth century. After publishing her most famous novel, *Blanca Sol* (1888), Cabello de Carbonara, said to be suffering from severe melancholy, was committed to an asylum outside of Lima, Peru.

The belief that women had to be protected from the dangers of literacy, a belief which in the Americas dates back to the time of the Spanish colonization—when novels were banned from the New World based on the dual assumption that they would mislead the indigenous populations and corrupt the women—still had currency in the earlier part of this century. Teresa de la Parra's novel, *Ifigenia* (1924), about a woman who wrote out of frustration and boredom with societal pressures and her limited choices as a woman, was criticized and censured in her native Venezuela, despite its critical acclaim abroad, on the grounds of posing a danger to women readers. Given this history, the very act of writing and the complementary act of reading were, and to some degree still are, subversive activities for Latin American women.

While Latin American societies have made great strides in improving conditions for women in this century, there still exists an alarmingly high rate of illiteracy, particularly among Black, mestiza, and Indian women. Even the relatively small number of women who have the advantages of an education and relative affluence, and choose to pursue writing, still face obstacles in publishing their work, often relying on smaller publishing houses with uneven distribution. Although some of the larger publishing houses have begun, in recent years, to include titles by women, hoping to duplicate the commerical success of writers such as Isabel Allende and Laura Esquivel, the notion that women's writing has limited appeal as opposed to the perceived universality of male authors is still all too common. This inequity in publishing sets off a domino effect, leading to fewer reviews, fewer works translated for foreign markets, and consequently less attention from scholars. This cycle is also reflected in the small number of women whose work is included in Latin American literature anthologies published in the United States. *The Borzoi Anthology of Latin American Literature, Vol. 2* includes only Clarice Lispector and Nelida Piñón among a total of thirty-eight fiction writers. *The Eye of the Heart: Short Stories from Latin America* raises the number to five of a total of forty-one authors: Gabriela Mistral, Maria Luisa Bombal, Dinah Silveira de Queiroz, Armonía Somers, and Clarice Lispector. The more recent *A Hammock Beneath the Mangoes* includes six stories by women in a collection of twenty-seven selections: Armonía Somers, Isabel Allende, Clarice Lispector, Lygia Fagundes Telles, Ana Lydia Vega, and Rosario Ferré.

The proliferation of anthologies dedicated to Latin American fiction could be largely accredited to the popularity of the "Boom" writers. In their works, readers discovered a very different kind of writing, one that played with language, created memorable characters in sometimes bizarre situations, and questioned our very notion of reality. Unfortunately, in the fanfare, women's writing was largely ignored. The present generation of women writers, however, do have predecessors. Writers such as Clarice Lispector, who wrote of the fantastic, and is just now being rediscovered; Rosario Castellanos, whose style and language made the landscape and people of her native state of Chiapas find a place in her readers' imagination; Lydia Cabrera, the Cuban anthropologist whose stories introduced the world to the "Magical Realism" that would years later become identified with the fiction of the "Boom" writers; Luisa Valenzuela, whose sophisticated work has drawn a steadily increasing audience; and Isabel Allende, whose books are repeatedly on the bestseller lists.

Because the twentieth century has witnessed such a large number of talented Latin American women writing fiction, to include them all is well beyond the scope of this book. It is intended, rather, to provide the reader with a selection of stories that reflect the richness and diversity of Latin American fiction being written by women, including younger, emerging voices. Some of the writers in this anthology, such as Rosario Ferré, Cristina Peri Rossi, Julieta Campos, and Elena Poniatowska, are more established; others, such as Vlady Kociancich, Magali García Ramis, and Barbara Jacobs, have already established solid reputations in Latin America and are just now being recognized in translation. In terms of themes, styles, and content, the stories selected represent a broad spectrum. Carmen Boullosa's "So Disappear" is in a stream of consciousness with a somewhat Gothic strain. Ferré's "Amalia" reveals parts of the puzzle bit by bit, with a first-person narration that is both captivating and haunting. Mastretta's "Aunt Elvira" is both a character study and an adventure tale with straightforward narration. Naranjo's "Over and Over" is also a combination of styles, narrating in detail the characters' daily activities as they listen to the radio, watch TV, and reminisce until they are joined by their friend, carrying her head in her arms. Two of the stories, by Jacobs and Yáñez, are monologues that reveal as much, if not more, about the narrator as they do about the subject being narrated. And Campos's story offers an exploration, through narrative, of the nature and possibilities of narrative itself.

The content of these stories is equally varied. Some deal with political issues, as does Peri Rossi's "The Annunciation," or with social and economic inequities as in Britton's "Death Lies on the Cots." Others, such as Kociancich's "A Family Man," deal with feelings of angst and regret. And yet others use the mundane to explore larger concerns, as does Yáñez's story, in which the narrator observes a neighbor as she negotiates sharing her kitchen with a mouse. In contrast to this, Eltit's story recounts the weight of the events of one crucial night, when the narrator danced for the head of John the Baptist. The all-too-fragile connection to reality is explored in Lubitch Domecq's "Bottles," and Hernández's "Teresa Irene" recounts the mythical nature and fate of a young girl, lending it the quality of a magical tale passed on from generation to generation.

The seventeen stories gathered here resist grouping, resist broad classification, and invite the reader to savor each of them individually. This anthology is intended only as a sampling of what is available, and judging from the productivity and talent of these writers, it is merely a glimpse of what is to come.

Out of the Mirrored Garden

S_o Disappear

CARMEN BOULLOSA

Come on! They're filthy. . . . Nobody can prove any different . . . filthy, noisy, absolutely crazy. And me?

I like to drink coffee alone, very slowly, lock myself in my room, look out at the terrace and see nothing on the horizon, nothing but sky (some sky, preferably a tiny fragment of sky, preferably gray) and forget about the damn racket that always, always, always makes its way through the wall the same way flies get around obstacles so that they always reach the light.

I like to walk the room as if it were impossible to count the steps needed to cross it, as if the room were as wide as the earth and fit in the palm of my hand. I hate them.

I've never seen them. Not once. I don't know what they look like but I know everything about them. I've learned to keep track of them. I can identify their steps, I know their moods at any given moment and I know perfectly—as if I could look into their minds— all the vile hatred they feel for me. As vile as they are.

No, they don't bathe. Ah, but even if they bathed, it wouldn't make any difference. Water can't dissolve soap against their hides; it slips and slides the way sand will never slip over water. They're so silly! When one sees them from far away, they might be what people generally call "good-looking," but our proximity makes me feel that they and good looks can't go together: their hair is teased and tangled and caked with who knows what against their clumsy heads, their socks have to be peeled from their feet like the skin from a potato. . . .

Ever since I arrived, they've been here. I have to admit, it took a while before I could identify them; at the beginning, I didn't know what they were. If I stayed shut up in my room, it wasn't because I didn't want to see them, but because that's the way I liked it, and if I've arrived here for good, it wasn't to be close to them. Still, I can't deny how much unites us now and how much has united us from the very first moment. The door opened up to me by the church ceremony slammed right in their faces.

I must have been very much in love with this man when I married him. I don't have much time to think about whether that's the case now or whether it was, but when it comes right down to it, I couldn't care less.

He comes every day. He arrives at night. He feeds off me, not like Dracula, reeking of celluloid; he literally feeds off me, voracious, never satiated. At noon he goes to restaurants and stuffs his face with the ridiculous words of businessmen disguised as academics and some underpaid cook's daily special.

I seldom think of him. If I don't reserve much space for him when I remember the two of us in the past—that past that others call happy—I leave him even less in the tedious present where the two of us are enveloped. Now I speak of him only because I believe I have to, if I want to make a more or less acceptable portrait.

(I said that he feeds off me because when I get up after having slept next to him, my body aches as if something had been extracted. Pain is like that. What they take away aches. What they leave you doesn't hurt a bit.

With them, on the other hand, I don't feel any pain. Is that why it doesn't occur to me to throttle them even though they're driving me nuts? Or have I not throttled them simply because I've never seen them? Or have I already throttled them?)

Tzak, tzak, tzak, they go. I hear them go tzak, tzak, tzak. Coming from them, the sound signifies terrible things. They curse all the tender leaves of all the innocent trees on earth. So why are they so angry?

My God! I'm always astonished by their inexhaustible capacity to hate everything.

Some of them think they've already gone. They think they aren't here anymore. Dreamers! Come on, I'm the only one who's where I shouldn't be and I know I can't leave; how could they flee? There's nowhere for them to go! They're horrible!

Not one of them has gone, I'm sure, because the noise, the noise they make just breathing, is ferocious. When I have breakfast staring at the blank wall, I sense them the way ants sense sugar, and they aren't even beside me, a wall divides us, separates us. Luckily, I'm far away from them.

What can they have done with the curtains I saw when I came in? Magnificent red drapes—so heavy they must soak up the dust. Some of them, or one of them, must have torn them down to dress up in and parade down the hall. And they think I'm the guilty one! I don't want to catch their germs!

I could poison them, but where do you buy poison? I can't cook. . . . I'm not very clever. . . . And after all, they're the ones that hate me, not me them. . . . Ha, they hate me. . . . What, don't they have anything else to think about? It's understood that I'd think about them. They worry me. But they're just children; they could well look the other way.

They dream the dreams of babies—that the night of their infancy has come to an end, that the cloud which keeps them child-sized evaporated when a huge sun came out and now they're allowed to open the doors of their house and go out into the street.

They'd like to be the bosses. They fantasize that they already are, that the place they live in has turned into something else.

Our dreams are diametrically opposed. I don't want any more than what I have, but if it would give me a little respite from their noise, I'd wish for them to live far away. Or not at all. Since they don't, I should let them come in to do my nails, my hair, to exchange the empty coffeepot for a full one . . .

The kids . . . They'd like to be far from here, running through fields, breathing pure air and being "big people," dull, dull grown-ups. . . . But running through fields, they'd end up destroying the young alfalfa with their boots; inhaling pure air, they'd exhale sticky smoke, like the fumes from burning plastic, and even if they were grown-up, the size of their bodies wouldn't change the fact that they'd still need to hold someone's hand crossing the street. . . . they'll never cross the street alone! They'll never know how to.

Ever since I arrived, there's been a trunk full of notes and old magazines in the bedroom. Every morning, I think I should throw it out. It's heavy and I know that if I want to get rid of it, I'll have to empty it, but the papers must be dirty and full of dust; I'd ruin my hands if I touched them. They keep watching me, watching, saying nothing: they're mute. I know they are, the way everything in the house is mute. The noises aren't words; pounding doesn't speak.

It's not the kids who come to serve me, to clean the room, bring the lovely hot coffee, the sweet rolls, the glorious bunches of fruit, and then take the dirty plates away, bring me a drink, and ask, "Can I get you anything else, ma'am?" They've never spoken to me about themselves. One even dared to recommend that I go out for a walk in the garden, arguing that it would be "good for your health" (mine, you understand). I lied so I wouldn't disappoint her; I said the sun was harmful to the skin and besides, I valued my pale complexion and treated it with the utmost care.

Sometimes I forget about them and they take drastic measures against me. "What, you don't want to hear us anymore?" they seem to say. "Here, take that, and that." They hurl their tiny bodies against the walls of my room.

I'm an adult. I feel bad about what they're doing. It isn't that it hurts me more than it hurts them, but it seems so senseless.

They'll hurt their ears! They'll ruin their little noses!

But I don't speak to them, it's enough to hear them from morning till night. Is it because I don't call or speak to them through the walls that they hate me so much?

Now I can hear them dragging something across the hardwood floor. They must be raising a fine dust that will rise from the boards, scoring the walls, tracing unconnected phrases with their absurd calligraphy. They've made the house a notebook in which they jot down their unbreatheable history.

They don't come into my room. I can't stop their noise. It arrives as a mirror, reflecting their eyes and acts, and who knows? I could be the one who invites it in.

They don't come into my room, but they've created a barricade around it with their insane and unyielding insanity.

Calm down, children. Relax. You won't get anywhere without tranquillity. You're losing all your chances of drawing closer to the doors and windows, or floating down a river that empties into the sea, or exchanging words among yourselves that have a beginning and an end. The only thing you're gaining is more and more and more lack of self-control. Calm down!

How long can the walls support the torrent? Who'd know?

An engineer could calculate the physical resistance, but the force that will break those walls down eventually can't be lifted onto a scale or held still to be measured. They come, they go, they jump. . . . When they fall to the floor in their fantasies, their bodies contract and explode. They disappear when anyone wants to touch them. They change from night to morning the way buds bloom or flowers die.

How many are there? How many? Do they call each other by name? I think they invent names to confuse each other. They know they must create confusion, that like branches loaded with leaves, they have to stand between the light source and earth's natural night, continuous night, austere night. . . .

They also say that for light to be light, it has to touch the atmosphere; if it didn't, it would stay on its crazy course without ever managing to shine. They don't want this contact, they want the natural darkness of light to persist; they don't want anything to touch it because with touching, it bursts or joyful light escapes, changing the dark symbol they defend into a friendly, ardent, living one.

. . .

They are the protectors of shadows, but if the shadows wanted to be on their side, they'd turn against them too. Why? They can't commit to anything.

Do they touch each other? I've spent hours listening to them, trying to decipher whether they touch each other or not. My question begins with "Do they see each other? Does each one know that there are many others like him, that the one he bumped into is someone just like him, deep down?"

I imagine them bumping, stumbling, running into each other and thinking, I bumped something, I ran into something, I stumbled, but never I bumped into someone, I ran into someone, I stumbled on someone. . . .

I'm afraid I'm boring you with all my pacing. I don't have any story to tell. Let's see: I'm a woman, I live shut up in this room (without a TV) by my own choice, because I feel like it. I'm married. I don't do anything special. I like to drink coffee. A bunch of kids from who-knows-where live around this room. Is one of them my child? It seems logical: female, married, why wouldn't I have kids?

To complete the picture, I'll say that I'm not having a bad time. They are, yes. They're suffering. Oh, how they suffer.

Now they're attacking again. There's no end to the stream of sounds that comes from their mouths.

I stick my head out the window. I try to count out loud so I won't hear them, but at the same time, I want to hear them. I don't understand what they're doing now. I've heard them moving things before, eating, fighting, hating, being cruel, getting dirtier, but I don't understand what they're doing today.

Where are they going? Why do they sound so active? They're insatiable.

I have nightmares. I think, I know them so well that I could have been one of them. I don't remember my mother or my father either. I want to stop the nightmare; I argue that I could never be one of them because—I'll spell it out, so that like magic, I'll be cured—I am a married woman, and if anyone were to study me, he wouldn't find a single worrisome trait in me.

Go on, it can't be that hard to stop dreaming about what one can't dream (I repeat, married woman, married woman).

It's true. In the silence that envelops the house when he arrives at night, everything is normal. They're quiet and everything asleep seems to be in order.

I smile then because I'm enjoying the farce. I think it's funny. I have a rather peculiar sense of humor.

A couple of days ago, I wrote "cruel." The idea was "They're cruel." I can read it in the laughter I hear now, because I know that they laugh while chasing after each other. Is it that I want to be with them, that I want to be in their games, and because I'm not, I think they're cruel?

No. Absolutely not.

Now what are they tossing around? What are they breaking? Destroying? And, above all, what is it that makes them laugh and laugh and laugh?

·   ·   ·

When the man of the house arrives, there's a sense of pause in the silence that he's not aware of because he doesn't look around him. He comes to bed like the shipwrecked sailor saved on an island, knowing that there is no salvation, only isolation, and in bed, although he closes his eyes and hangs on to me like a child, he hardly touches me, the way one touches the fleeting image of an enigmatic fantasy.

Don't be bored! Don't fall asleep on me! I don't want to overwhelm you with everything I feel! Keep listening. Believe me, I'm going to tell you something terrible so that you won't abandon the slow pace of this story. Listen: I panic when the branches of the trees scrape against the window. Why? Because it sounds like they're doing something awful, as if to tell me as they pass through the house, above and below, that they're carrying some corpse. Are they dying? I'm not talking about the branches, you understand. I'm talking about the ones who make noise all through the morning and all day while at night, to deceive the man of the house, just to deceive him, they keep quiet.

They're like an open, occupied sepulchre, like a rotting body, a body that sounds like it's rotting. Are they dying? I don't know.

Are they walking through the house dead? I don't know. What are they carrying? They never get tired of hating, hating, hating. They never consider what they could do with their boring hatred.

I'm afraid of them, but that doesn't change the fact that in the morning while I have my coffee, the pleasure is mine.

When else do I laugh? I laugh when I manage to cut short the never-ending dreams and untangle my hands and head from the sheets; then I laugh, "It's over!" I think of the dream, and I see it approach again, unstoppable as the sea, and no matter how much I think I'm spending too many hours sleeping, I can't escape, and it climbs, climbs, climbs. . . . It floods the bed and hauls me off by the feet until I'm sunk, asleep again. Later, I free myself once more, and laugh "It's over!" I laugh a lot every morning, each time I think I'm finally going to wake up.

I talked about their caked hair against their lowing, childish heads, about their filthy ears and their disgusting socks stuck to their feet like potato skins. I'm saying it again so that you'll believe me. It wasn't a rhetorical statement, it's the truth.

They say I ought to do something about it. In their dreams, I speak sweetly to them, kneel before them and wash them, change their clothes, patiently comb their hair. I never will.

"On your mark . . . get set . . . go!"

They're getting ready.

What'll they do now? What were they preparing for?

When I opened the sugar bowl this morning, I thought they'd come out, rise up from between the lumps like a colony of ants.

The children aren't inoffensive, I'm sure. I'm afraid of them. I'm afraid to say it. OK, how on earth do I know they're children? I've never seen them! I always forget.

How do they picture me? In slippers with a long flannel nightgown? Good outfit for a warrior. At any rate, be afraid of me, be very afraid of me. Because if they are dark birds vulnerable to death, I am a twister that carries earth and seeds to the fields, that breaks windows, tears off doors and takes them . . . where? I turned out the way a twister turns out, and someday I could be sitting next to you.

There are days like today, when I think I'm a flame, consuming, devastating, devouring what surrounds me. So I think I'll finish him and the children off, the house and all it contains, I'll do away with the sticky hatred and all the phantoms it drags along with it, including me.

But I don't know whether to think that I too will vanish, that I might turn to look at myself in the mirror and not be there anymore.

I think about it often; when I need to calm down, I put my defenseless face into the hungry cloud of fire. It calms me and helps me to relax, but inside I can't stop the voice that keeps telling me "disappear then, just disappear."

Translated by Heidi Neufeld Raine

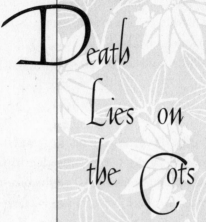

Death Lies on the Cots

*Death lies on the cots
the lumpish mattresses
the black blankets.*

RESIDENCE ON EARTH

—PABLO NERUDA

ROSA MARIA
BRITTON

M other's name?"
"What did you say?"

"What is your mother's family name?"

"Martínez. My name is Ana Berta Martínez. My mother's name is Eulalia Martínez Rico de Ocú, province of Herrera."

"Then what is your father's name, Señora? We must have all the information complete."

"My father's name was Encarnación González, but I don't go by his name."

The blood drips down between her legs until it reaches the floor, and, embarrassed, she brings her feet together so no one will notice the dark stains. Before leaving the house she had stuffed several pieces of towel between her legs, but it is not enough to hold back the dark torrent coming from her body.

"Your identity card number?"

"I don't remember it very well. I left home this morning and forgot to bring it with me."

"Everyone knows they always have to bring the I.D. to the hospital and still you all keep forgetting it."

"I know, Señora, but . . ."

"Of course, I see. But that's no excuse. . . . You have to realize that this card is to be carried with you at all times. Where were you born, and what was the date?"

"In Ocú, Señora. February twenty-fourth, nineteen fifty-five. I'll be thirty this year.

Her whole body aches, and she imagines she sees a multicolored halo around the head of the secretary making out the registration form.

. . .

"What brings you to Emergency?"

"I feel so bad, Señora, and I'm bleeding down below. Since last night—"

"And you didn't come before this? It's three in the afternoon."

"I've been here since ten o'clock, waiting for my turn, but the other secretary who left already told me to sit down, that they would call me right away, and . . ."

"And you just sat there in a daze because you didn't have your form made out? How do you expect us to take care of you if you haven't even registered? Have you been here before?"

"Yes. I had an operation four weeks ago. In Ward Nineteen. They took out my uterus."

"Didn't you bring your hospital records number? We'll have to find your file. No doctor is going to want to look at you without your medical history. Do you remember the number that was on it?"

She feels something throbbing sluggishly in the middle of her belly, and she would like to stretch out on the floor. Her weariness is gradually softening up her bones and without surprise she watches the red spot growing at her feet. With sluggish steps she goes to sit down in a corner by the wall, certain that they will never find her medical records, and resigned to waiting for her turn. By this time Marisol must be home from school and taking care of the little one. Things are not so bad, since she left enough milk and some money in the tin can where she is certain her daughter will have discovered it. Even at nine, Marisol is able to cook and wash clothes, and does a good job.

All the time she was in the hospital the girl had been in charge of the house. Thanks to a neighbor woman who took care of her little brother during the mornings, she was able to keep going to school.

Ana Berta closes her eyes and leans against the wall. Everything is spinning around her. Oh, God—if they could only find her records soon, because she can't last much longer.

"Don't worry, it's nothing, dear. These things sometimes happen after an operation like this," she had told Marisol that morning when she saw the fear on her daughter's face as she got a look at the bedding soaked in the red liquid. "Hurry, now, you're going to be late for school. Here's forty centavos for the bus and something to eat at noon." She tried to avoid the girl's inquisitive look as she handed over the money. Hadn't she just told her the evening before that she would have to get up early in order to walk to school because there wasn't a bit of money in the house?

She watched Marisol as she carefully put on her dress; her only uniform was already shiny from so much ironing. And how carefully she took care of it. She always hung it on a hook, where it would not get damp from the rain. The corrugated zinc sheets that Manuel José had managed to get hold of seemed to have more and more holes lately, and sometimes it seemed as if it were raining harder inside the house than it did outside. But it was hers! Even though it was just four walls made of cinder blocks set sloppily on top of each other, with a corrugated metal roof over the little slab of cement. At least it didn't have a dirt floor like so many others in the neighborhood did. Manuel José had built it when things had been going well between them. She was carrying Rafaelito in her belly when they finished it. She still wasn't sure what had happened: her man had a good job in a paint factory, he was supporting them well enough, and suddenly he went off the deep end over a woman in the neighborhood. When she complained, he had left without even saying good-bye. She went to look for him at the factory and even had to get several court orders so he would come through with the child support for Rafaelito and Carlos, who were his children. At first he had paid without hesitation, but later on he changed jobs and it was really hard to find him. Now it shamed her to go to the district court all the time to put in her claim, along with so many others like herself.

"They look like buzzards waiting for those poor guys," she had heard one of the supervisors at the paint factory remark while she was waiting one day for Manuel José to appear with the money. She and many others in the same situation . . .

But what else could she do? With three babies, one of them still breastfeeding, where was she going to find a job? Not with any family; the first condition they insisted on was there should be none of this going to school, and the only day off would be Sunday—and then only if the lady of the house wasn't giving a little party. Like that first job she had, when she first got to town; they would never let her go out, and she nearly died of boredom in that prison. And then her mistress loudly denounced her ingratitude, made such an angry fuss and even refused to pay her when she announced she was leaving. Later on she learned a little better just how things were, and no one ever made such a sap of her again. She was no longer the timid *cholita* with long black hair and butterflies in her stomach who had arrived from Ocú riding a small, rickety bus, more frightened than anything. Back in Los Llanos she had left her mother dying of old age at forty, with three little brothers, poverty and hunger always snapping at their heels. Her stepfather used to work the earth from sunup to sundown, making thirty cents a day selling cassava and yams, only to spend it all in the cantina. He didn't stop drinking until he was out cold on some sidewalk, stinking of urine. Then, with his basket empty, he would come back to their hut in a bad mood, ready to pick a fight with anyone who crossed him. And one day she couldn't stand it any longer and borrowed some money to get away to the capital. A cousin got her first job for her, with the mistress who was always having parties on Sundays. Later on she learned how to dress and put on makeup. She cut her hair, got a perm, and when she went back to her village for the *Manito* festival, her mother hardly recognized her she was so changed, with her hair dyed red.

That was when she met Marisol's father, he seemed like such a nice guy, a good dancer, and what a line! She was never sure what it was Rafael did for a living, but he was always well dressed and had money in his pocket. When she went back to the city he began to call her at work. On her days off they went dancing at the Cosita Buena or else to the movies if she had to get back early. It was to the sound of the accordion that their romance blossomed and culminated in her swollen belly. Her mistress kicked her out when she realized what was going on, and it wasn't until later that she discovered she had a right to appeal, but it was too late then. And Rafael? It was hello and good-bye! When she went to tell him what the situation was, he dropped her right then and there, and treated her as if she were some common whore. Oh, the pain she suffered over the whole affair.

"Señora Martínez, Señora Martínez," the voice reaches her from far away. She opens her eyes as she senses the secretary beside her and realizes she has been dozing. She pulls at the skirt squeezed between her thighs and becomes aware of the dampness rising stickily over her abdomen.

"Señora Martínez, do you recall what date you were operated on? We can't find your records without the number."

"It was four weeks ago, around the fifth of April," she answers in a feeble voice. "Yes, that's right, I'm certain, it was April fifth."

"Do you recall the name of the doctor who performed the operation?"

"Yes, it was Dr. Hidalgo, a tall, heavy man, he was the one who operated on me. He was very nice."

"We'll call him to see if he wants to come and take care of you." The secretary looks at her in alarm when she sees the red patch on the floor. She returns to her post behind the desk, glancing out of the corner of her eye at the woman seated in the corner, head against the wall, who seems to be sleeping again.

Later on she would see Rafael here and there at dances and even once in Ocú, but he would turn his face away, as if he had never known her. She went to her village to have the baby because she had nowhere else to go. Her stepfather gave her a hard time and wanted to kick her out of the house when he found out she was pregnant, but her mother came to her defense and allowed her to hang her hammock in a corner until Marisol was born. Then she went back to the city to work, but she had learned the lesson that Rafael's shamelessness had taught her. Ana Berta worked hard during those months. She mailed every cent home to the village so her daughter wouldn't lack for anything, and forgot the Cosita Buena and the Saturday night dances. She met Manuel José by accident.

He was working on some construction near her house, and every time she went by there on her way to get something at the store, he would whistle at her and flirt, and without being aware of it, she would accentuate the swaying of her hips. She dyed her hair again and got a perm. Manuel José invited her out, and took her to La Chorrera, to the house of a friend who was having a birthday. The latter was a pleasant, homey sort of man who kept making remarks as if she and Manuel José were already going together.

"Look out, Manuel José, these women from Ocú really get jealous; they're pretty, but very jealous. Compadre, I can see you're already hog-tied and rough-locked, ain't nothin' gonna help you."

And Manuel José proudly squeezed her hand and caressed her shoulder. She knew she looked good in those white pants and tight sweater, and fell in love again.

"I've got a two-year-old daughter in Ocú that my mother is taking care of," she confessed one afternoon when he had taken her to the movies and proposed that they live together.

"I'm building a little place in Tocumen, Ana Berta, and I want you to be my woman."

Those were good years. She had no complaints. She went home to the village to pick up the girl and bring her back. How happy Marisol had been to get away from the hut with its stench of smoke and urine. The old man had had an attack of some sort and couldn't get out of the hammock, so now it was her mother and her nearly grown brothers who scratched around in the earth, looking for something to keep them alive. Manuel José was a hard worker, that she couldn't deny. Always in a good mood, he didn't go out drinking on the weekends like the other men, except now and then. They moved to Tocumen, to the half-finished house, and it was a good thing it was summertime, because they had to sleep on cardboard boxes without a roof for a long time until Manuel José was able to get hold of some secondhand sheets of corrugated metal roofing and the remaining cinder blocks to finish the walls. They had the good fortune of having an outhouse close by and a common water-faucet that their representative had gotten installed.

Manuel José had a permanent job at the paint company, with a monthly wage of two hundred fifty balboas a month, which wasn't bad. No, no, she had no complaints during those six years they were together. He behaved, and he became quite attached to Marisol. He treated her just like a daughter, even after his own children, Rafaelito and Carlos, were born. Manuel José never knew why she had insisted so on the name of the first boy. It was a nostalgic gesture; though she didn't tell him about it, she still had the memory of Rafael stuck in her mind—the dancer, the partygoer with the easy smile and the flirting remark. Manuel José was so different, so concerned about the house, about the roof, about the wood to build a bed—which really looked so nice to her—but never, never did he have any time for distractions or for dancing, although they did go occasionally. Oh, and how furious he got when she bought the little radio with the money from some lottery tickets. It was a miracle he didn't break it. . . .

"Ana Berta Martínez, Room Eleven."

The clock hanging halfway up on the flaking wall shows five o'clock in the afternoon and she worries whether Marisol will have given the bottle to the baby yet. The voice that reaches her so insistently from so far away is repeating her name. She recalls her village and, without knowing why, she doesn't want to see the doctor anymore; nothing hurts her now, and they'll probably just get mad at her.

"Ana Berta Martínez . . . Ana Berta Martínez . . . Room Eleven."

"Señora, they're calling you." Someone beside her touches her arm and she gets up knowing that she will leave a trail of dark blood on the floor which has just been negligently mopped after the secretary complained about the spots all over it.

Her neighbors had warned her in good time about what was going on with Manuel José and the woman who eventually carried him off. They had begun riding to work together on the Tocumen-Cathedral bus line when they left early in the morning, and she looked so stuck-up wearing some company's uniform and wearing high heels and makeup as though she were off to a party at that time of day, smelling of a kind of perfume that had nothing to do with keeping house.

Later on they were arriving together in the evening, and he would walk with her to her place, which was some distance from the bus stop. All their comings and goings were recounted in the most minute detail, even the moment when Manuel José was seen putting his arm around the waist of that slut and keeping it there until they got to her house, located in the area on the other side of the highway, which already had cement sidewalks and sewer drains.

She protested, oh yes, she complained, screaming and shouting, and he just got angry and left the house. He returned very late, drunk, for the first time, and with the bad temper of someone who is in the wrong and knows it. They didn't speak for a week. She served him his meals with the radio of discord turned up full blast, eager to drown out her thoughts. The squabbles over the other woman went on for six months, and finally the other woman prevailed and snatched him away.

"You are Ana Berta Martínez, right?" the woman dressed in white asks, looking at her impatiently. "We've been calling you for a good while now, Señora. Didn't you hear? Come with me."

She takes her by the arm, for the first time becoming aware of the dark trail flowing like a river from beneath the woman's skirt.

"Why didn't you let anyone know you were bleeding this way?" she scolds with a preoccupied air, touching the coldness in the other's flesh with her practiced hand.

The judge set her child support at forty dollars per month and at first Manuel José paid up. Every two weeks he handed over the money at the door of the factory, his hands sweaty, without looking her in the face.

"You should be satisfied I let you have my house," he told her that day when she dared to complain to him because he hadn't given her the full amount.

When he changed jobs she never caught up with him again, no matter how many orders she got from the district court. Someone eventually told her he had married the other woman legally, and so she went over to the other side of the highway looking for him in the tangle of buildings that all seemed alike, but no one could tell her anything about the woman in high heels and the blue-and-white uniform.

With no job and no money, how could she take care of the children? The owner of the little store provided the solution when she went to ask him for credit. Out behind the storeroom, on some rough sacks that smelled of rice, dust, and rat droppings, the man relieved himself quickly and gave her three balboas and a soup bone. Afterward, it was another guy who worked in the gas station, right there in the ladies' bathroom, and that was the way it went. But never in her home, never! Never on the wooden bed with its thick cotton blanket that Manuel José had bought her and she now shared with Marisol. The two boys slept in the hammock. Some of her neighbors, when they realized the way things were going, stopped speaking to her, as if their own poverty had not taken away their right to judge others.

At the health center they told her they couldn't operate on her so she wouldn't have more children because she was still too young. Well, she was twenty-eight going on sixty! Or at least it felt that way sometimes. Still, they put something inside her, saying it was to keep her from getting pregnant again, but it was in vain; in six months she had another swollen belly. It was a difficult pregnancy. Manuel José had been sending them money from time to time through a friend who refused to tell her where he was so she wouldn't bother him. But as soon as the friend discovered she was pregnant, he stopped coming around. She might have had the baby there in the house had it not been for the neighbor, who took her to the hospital.

The little nobody's child was born at eight months, skinny and sickly. It was after the birth that the hemorrhages began and she'd had to go to the health center, where they referred her to the hospital. How scared she was when that doctor told her she needed to be operated on for a tumor. It must have been some venereal disease she had, and they hadn't wanted to tell her. She went to La Chorrera, looking for Manuel José's friend to get him to help her with the children while she was in the hospital. The man received her coldly; all those jokes about the women of Ocú were now forgotten. He denied having seen his friend for some time, with the lie appearing on his lips like a flower, and contempt in his eyes. His wife was more considerate and gave her ten balboas that out of a sense of pride she should have not accepted—but who said the poor could afford luxuries like that?

She sent her boys to their grandmother in the village, for the old woman was now alone in the hut since the death of the old man. Ana Berta's brothers were already married, but they lived nearby. The boys would at least have food there, with their grandmother, because it wasn't going so badly with her little harvest of cassava and yams and her chickens.

"Mama, I have to have an operation. Take care of the boys and I promise to send you some money as I get better. I've got a job and everything."

She lied in the note she had given the bus driver, who promised to drop the boys off at Ocú at the house of some relatives who could take them to Los Llanos. *(Mama, don't worry about me, life has treated me badly, worse than it did you. . . . Take care of the boys. . . .)*

. . .

"Doctor, this woman is bleeding terribly. You should take care of her now. I'm going to put her in Room Eleven for examination."

She feels the hands that help her undress and the goose bumps rise up on her skin with the cool breeze from the air-conditioning. She thinks she sees an expression of surprise on the face which, bending over her, helps remove the panties, and is ashamed for them to see her this way, altogether filthy, the sticky liquid dripping down her thighs. The nurse's aide removes the pieces of towel from between her legs and throws them in the pail. If they could at least allow her to go to the bathroom and wash . . .

The operation took place on a Tuesday at noon, after they had nearly killed her by several hours' starvation. They stuck so many needles into her and gave her so many enemas that her butt was burning. She had understood nothing about what they were doing to her, as now, lying flat on this stretcher with a light shining in her face and a young doctor looking at her eyes with a smaller light. And she has the urge to scream out that that isn't where she is bleeding, that she is dying, as she was then, with the needles in her arms and the blood dripping little by little; was it then? no, now, not then . . .

She got out in three weeks, weak as a newborn cat, but happy to be out of that place alive, with its smell of disinfectant soap and the nurses always eager to call you lazy if you complained even the slightest bit. Marisol, the poor kid, stayed at home taking care of the baby, with the help of some neighbors, who suddenly recovered their sense of humanity. Of course, the money she left for her was hardly enough for anything at all, but they managed. When she returned, there was no gas left for cooking; the small tank she had gotten from the owner of the little store had hardly lasted at all. And now that she had just had her operation, from whom would she get another one?

Dr. Hidalgo reaches her side, and she sees him through a haze. Why is he looking at her like that, almost angrily? He touches her belly which is burning so hotly from within, as if a furnace had been turned on there. They open her legs and she feels the cold instrument being pushed inside her like a drill.

"Please, Doctor, gently . . . please. Doctor!" she is screaming silently. Don't hurt me like that brute last night, who nearly killed me. . . . What are you asking me, Doctor? I know I'm all torn up inside after you did such a good job on me. I'm bleeding, and you can't do a thing about it, is that it, Doctor? Don't get angry with me, no matter how much you want to. Why did I do it? You ask why did I have sex when you warned me that I shouldn't do anything at all for at least six months? Is that what is worrying you, Doctor? My world is coming to an end, I already know that. . . . Why do you ask that young man with such a wise look on his face if he wasn't even there to see it? Oh God . . . To say that all women are just all pigs . . . Oh God, my children, I'm dying . . . What will happen to them? And you still wonder why I did it? It was for six dollars, Doctor, for six dollars.

Translated by Leland H. Chambers

Allegories

JULIETA
CAMPOS

There are stage sets which by themselves tell a story. Places that, on being described, narrate themselves. Such, for example, is the half-glimpsed interior of a Venetian palace before whose door a liveried servant appears, buttoning his waistcoat with his left hand: Count Uccello dwells there, a descendant of one of the doges. In Venice every palace is a stage that evokes the histrionics of Wagner and the sumptuous melancholy of the Palazzo Guistiniani. Thick curtains of red velvet and red tapestries with a majestic fall, moderately in disrepair, will accentuate the atmosphere of confinement and favor the tepid eroticism that must have flowed, by virtue of the intercession of Mathilde Wesendonk's golden pen, throughout the second act of *Tristan*.

Isn't the whole city, after all, the most undisguised and lavish stage set ever?

The redness of the exterior walls bares itself here and there, suggesting the inner life of the residence, with a certain refined immodesty. Until just recently there were three people living in the house, but the young nephew of the count has gone away. The count spends his days in the tiny garden that opens onto the Square of the Archangels. A faltering ivy, now amber, covers that back side of the palace which looks out over the garden: a diminutive jungle of orange trees, jasmine, lupines, thorn-laden roses unpruned now for a long while, savage, intrusive weeds that no one pulls out, tiny invading flowers overflowing the carefully outlined beds, cats that settle in some protected place and stay there in discreet silence for two or three months. The count devotes long periods to leafing through albums of paintings, and he goes out only to the Accademia from time to time, where, with infinite patience, through a gold-mounted lens supported by a cupid's figure, he examines the *Allegories* of Bellini. In the museum he is greeted with respect, and they try to leave him alone so that he can contemplate at leisure the man emerging from the seashell who is himself contemplating the serpent. When the count appears, the tourists become a little uneasy, uncertain if they should applaud or not, divining the appearance onstage of an actor of old repute, unjustly forgotten. On occasion, he comes to a halt for a few moments in the adjoining salon, before *La Tempèsta*, and then, after casting a final gaze at his *Allegories*, he quickly leaves as if time were pressing on him, crosses the bridge, and without swerving goes straight toward the red palace which, half opening to devour its owner, emits the iridescent and tremulous luminosity of a seashell by virtue of the sun's reflections multiplied by the beveled panes of the windows, by the rays that fall into the numerous mirrors, and the varied glimmerings sent forth by the Murano lamps. So as not to mention the departed nephew, the lord and his servant speak of roses and head colds, say the neighbors. The same neighbors thought they had spotted the young man on the third floor balcony or descending to the garden by way of the open stairs that connect all the levels of the house on the outside, but they soon realized that it was only the servant dressed in the clothing of the heir apparent, and the most observant of them pointed out that he had waved his hair and lightened it one or two shades to emphasize the resemblance. The count's age is uncertain: those who have seen him up close ascribe near elderliness or near youthfulness to him, without being able to determine the basis for their uncertainty concerning the passage of time in that beautiful face, that profile from an ancient coin, those intense, evasive eyes, those mannerisms either brisk or excessively fatigued. Those who pass before the little garden gate at the same time every day find it strange to see him constantly in the same position, motionless, with a pen in his hand; and while there are those who assume he is writing long letters to the one who has so inopportunely absconded, others would swear that he is not writing but sketching, attempting to reproduce from memory, perhaps, the allegory of the man emerging from the seashell and contemplating the serpent. In this way his visits to the Accademia are justified, those excursions that for brief periods uproot him from his disquieting self-absorption. With more envy than sympathy they attribute a useless fortune to him, swollen because of his new widower's state (by the grace of a Neapolitan spouse so generous that she must have left him both free and unpardonably rich at the same time) as well as an egotistic vein that had never altered even in the company of the only son of his sister, deceased at the same time as his wife.

The count appears in the garden during the mornings, when the musicians of the Phoenix begin to rehearse the overture to *The Phantom Ship* which will soon initiate the winter music season. There awaits him a willow armchair with flowered cretonne cushions, now rather discolored, a Scotch-style woolen blanket, and a small table. The rains eventually displace him to the covered terrace. But his figure has mimicked the melancholy aura of the little wild garden, and he has become so consubstantial with it that the day-to-day passersby think they can make him out behind the encrusted verdure of the hedge as they peer through the grating of the indiscreet little gate, even though the willow chair is not visible and a light, chilling breeze suggests a heavy rain shower to come soon. In a café far away from the Square of the Archangels, they talk of an empty gondola seen at Isola Bianca, where no one goes anymore since the bones of the ancient guests of San Michele Cemetery were incinerated there and where now, it is rumored with a certain emphasis that suggests repugnance as much as it does fascination, only snakes prosper. The count's gondola is no longer a gondola like the rest: the farther away from the palace the story gets told, and by folks who have never seen the protagonist in person, the drearier the gondola becomes and the more ambiguous the image of its owner. Both of them, by this time almost phantomlike, have been detected on one of the small, low islands of the periphery, those uninhabited, marshy, disquieting mirrors of the city where the earth and the water do not respect their mutual limits and are blended in the lead-colored, quivering, irresolute mud. When the fog settles and the whole city seems to rise in it as if it were about to take flight, or, with even the support of its foundations seeming to yield, as if on the point of giving way without resistance to the avid embrace of the sea; when the bridges and staircases slippery with moss that descend to the livid waters of the interior canals are not to be distinguished from the fog in that milky, undifferentiated murk; when the darkish red of the interior of Venice is fermenting in that misty, humid vapor, and the marble of Venice's façade is scattering in an ashy spume so that the city-island turns into its own mirage and floats suspended above the lake, rose-colored, unreal, now nearly vanished—the count has been seen simultaneously in San Trovaso, in the field of Santa Margherita, in San Rocco, in Santos Giovanni e Paolo, and in Santa Maria Formosa, in the Frari and Santo Zanipolo. Sometimes they speak of his death: his servant had discovered him in his bedroom the morning after, beaten about the head with a silver candelabrum by someone unknown; or of his disappearance: no one has seen him since that afternoon on that bridge or that little alleyway, with his black umbrella opened out in spite of the fact that it was scarcely drizzling. Stories are attributed to him whose authenticity is sufficiently confirmed but whose protagonists are always someone else. The truth is that the count has vanished and it is useless to look through the grating to peer at him in his garden (but it is also true that winter is approaching and that the fog and the glacial wind lend themselves to cruelty). It is a fact that he has stopped frequenting the Accademia. Neither the *Allegories*, which are near the entrance, nor the Giorgione in the adjoining salon has called for his maniacal, scrupulous contemplation. The cardinal's purple on the palace walls, purified by the rain, seems to take upon itself an atmosphere of bereavement that is not exclusive to the palace nor to those walls, because every winter the whole of Venice bewails its grief like a chorus of hired mourners, but the neighbors prefer to attribute this to the disappearance of the count in order to isolate the trappings of mourning there, as they used to brick up the doorways of houses where victims had died of the plague in the so-called Dark Ages: an ostentatious show of mourning on the most dilapidated façades as well as on those that, with some reticence, conceal the proximity of death.

A note worthy of the tabloids but indubitably ingenious nonetheless is due to an assiduous devotee of grappa at a gathering that meets every Sunday afternoon in the bar around the corner of the palace, a modest establishment that some jokester had baptized "The Palace of Minos": the servant had removed the body at dawn and gone to throw it into the sea, or, better, had left it unburied on Isola Biance, where everybody knows the serpents swarm. Since the weather is cold, the rain does not cease, and life in Venice is so provincial that stories bearing a vampirish stamp are welcome to break the monotony. And to think that the truth is so much simpler and that merely allowing the stage set to narrate itself would suffice to be able to read it: violating the memory stamped in the mirrors and fastening down like butterflies on pins the words which the wind has gradually interwoven among the indecisive flowerings of the Murano lamps.

There must have appeared then a third character ("until just recently there were three . . . but the young nephew of the count had gone away . . ."). No, it was not the servant, who in the true story is an obscure walk-on, but a young English girl who must have arrived in Venice at the close of summer and after a few days had moved to the Palazzo Uccello, which that autumn would become acquainted with the intermittent florescence of one clandestine, dizzying love affair, impatient and hasty, written upon another one. The furtive couple slipped away very early one morning through the narrow grating of the gate to the square, and went toward the nearest landing, where the youthful pair took the vaporetto coming from the Lido bound for the Santa Lucia station. From the scene that had been acted out the evening before, a good while after nightfall, there were also discovered, besides the three characters who mime the outline of this Venetian episode, the reddish hangings that the count's grandparents had ordered installed when Wagner brought them into fashion, around the autumn of 1858; the mirrors, the only other survivors of the 1800s together with the lacquered secretary and the portrait of his great-aunt painted by Rosalba Carriera and the oversized lamps rocked perilously by the wind from the lagoon, accomplices in the secret that was always to be preserved around the agitated words, the intemperate reproaches alluding to lies and madness, to betrayals, to mortal wounds, to jealous scenes—and, in a word, blending the intemperateness of the words with the harmonious melody that fine moistened crystalware puts forth when awakened by a skillful hand or the wind.

But who would this reading suffice? Because the noise of all that verbal exuberance and the melodramatic uproar of the pantomime's broad gesturing might be overlooked forever if one did not read between the lines the violent buried anguish of another discourse not uttered: "Who will ever reveal the secret and bottomless cause of all my grief?" (the beginning of a long, sad lament directed by King Mark to his nephew, taken from the garden scene in Act Two of *Tristan and Isolde*).

As an augury, the Giorgione in the Accademia, with its strange garden colors beneath leaden afternoons when electrical storms draw near, must have transmitted its premonitory innuendo to the count. Now that the summer has already begun, it does not seem strange to anyone, in fact it is the most natural thing in the world, that the windows above the garden have been opened once more and that the same servant who is batting the blinds with an oversized feather duster should afterward appear at the door that opens unto the canal, buttoning his waistcoat with his irreproachably gloved left hand. The count, in a willow chair, is writing in a notebook and, though it is beginning to get hot, covers his legs with the Scottish blanket. He writes in order to summon up, by turning it into words, an inopportune recollection: "There are certain gloomy afternoons when it seems the entire world is on the verge of coming to an end."

Translated by Leland H. Chambers

Ice Cream

ELENA
CASTEDO

The ice cream Turk! The ice cream Turk's here!" Voices, running steps, and barks startled the warm morning. From his perch between me and the wagon, my master primed his burly mustache with his hairy fingers, took his soft hat off, dusted it against his thigh, and put it back on carefully. Not a good sign; his primping conjured unbearably long, unscheduled waits. Oases like the one we were now approaching—visible in the distance because of the profusion of palm trees, pines, and an oak or two surrounding houses long as trains—were not my favorite stops. Too often one of those fancy ladies in suede riding outfits, or flowing pantaloons and big hats, came floating out of the heady-smelling gardens and displayed no interest whatsoever in any of the treasures that came out of our wagon; they only observed my master. In a cloud of flower scents, the fancy ladies then floated back and disappeared beyond their gates and tall walls, down some path lined with rosebushes, and into some garden building. Too often my master soon followed suit, and there was I, under the weight of the wagon and the hot sun, planted on the road's barren dirt, not a blade of grass or weed, not a drop of water, nothing to do but wiggle my tongue around the metal in my dry mouth, bend one leg for a while, then bend another leg, let gas out, and watch the insufferable flies laugh at my attempts to scare them with my hide's tremors. I was in no mood for that, in fact my knees were about to give up.

Most of our stops were among clusters of houses or villages. Sometimes a peasant flagged us from the side of the road. These were chances to cool my hooves, and wiggle my hide to soothe the spots on my ribs where the pole-holding leather strap caused sweating and tingling. I also always hoped for a candy, or a sugar cube, or even an ice cream to fall close enough for me to scoop it up in a hurry, or for some nice pats on the neck to shake the dust, or a friendly scratch on my prickly mane. It was also mildly entertaining to observe the people so excited about getting ice cream, or considering and sometimes buying items. But after a while it got boring and I was rearing to go again. The truly deluxe stops were when we arrived at eateries. My master got off and stayed inside them for a good while. At the back they had troughs or an old bathtub with water, bins with hay, usually some grass, and—unless my master was in a foul mood—he un-hitched the wagon off me. Ahhh, then I stretched and bent as I pleased, rubbed itchy spots against a handy surface, and tail-hit pesky flies with a vengeance; oh, it felt wonderful. And if luck was really with me, there was another horse there, or nearby, for some social-izing, or even more delicious nuzzling.

Shhhhh, my master said unnecessarily when we arrived in front of the gates surrounding these lush gardens. He never had to use the reins on me, and if he did, it was just to show off, because I knew perfectly well when to stop and when to go. Many people flocked to us, mostly women, some in black with white aprons, some in uni-forms of pastel colors, some in old colorless frocks, and also some sweaty men with no shirts and rolled-up pants from working in the gardens, or in the granary. The crowd milled around, observing our dusty blue wooden wagon. Those who knew how to read the curving letters on the sides and back told the others slowly, *"La palomita patriótica,"* "The Patriotic Little Dove," and underneath, *"Todo lo indispensable para un hogar feliz,"* "All the necessities to make a happy home." And in one corner near the roof, they read the ribbon cross-ing a golden cone with a purple dome, *"Helados!"* "Ice cream!" in pink letters.

"No, *niño,* there's no dove in the wagon," a mother told her transfixed child, "no, not a very white lady either."

"Just that big fellow with a mass of mustache and eyebrows, and the big belt?"

"Just him, the ice cream Turk."

A young woman in uniform who observed our wagon with wide eyes was told by an older one, "This Turk brings loads of things to sell, some cheaper than Don Miguel at the trading post, some not, but he's got something nobody else has, nobody: he's got ice cream!" The wide-eyed younger one twitched all over, smiling nervously.

My master came down, tilting the wagon as he hit the metal step, disturbing the balance on my spine. He opened the doors and started to hand out paper cones with purple balls that glistened in the sun, and to deposit money in his belt pouch. Children, realizing they had to pay to get this marvel, took a few steps backward. Some ran frantically down the road, looking back from time to time. Some went to slouch and press their worn, dark clothes against the wall surrounding the gardens, or against a tree. They played without interest with a stick or a sling, observing the scene from the corner of their eyes. My master busily showed fabrics, thread spools, dyed wool, bottles of cologne and flu syrup, aspirin, cotton dresses, wooden mortars, paper and envelopes, girdles, kites, ladles, a harmonica, combs, brooms. . . . Birds that had flocked away came back and waited up in the trees, perhaps for some spilled rice, or in case I provided them with some dung with seed in it.

Two fancy ladies arrived at the iron gates and stood behind them, observing us and telling the dogs to hush. A fancy child came running out of the long house and asked one of the two fancy ladies if she could have ice cream. "Of course not, my treasure," the fancy lady answered, "you know very well we can eat only the ice cream served at the houses of friends."

"Or at the Waldorf," the other fancy lady said, "or the Little Chocolate Negro, or any of the good confectionery shops downtown."

"Why?" the child complained.

"Because this ice cream may be contaminated and give you typhoid fever. You can have ice cream when school starts and we go back," the fancy lady promised.

"Ugh, I don't want to go back to school," the fancy child screeched, and ran through the garden back to the long house.

"One time, when I was Jesusita's age," one of the fancy ladies told the other one, "during the siesta, I sneaked out of the house and bought street vendor's ice cream. Then I agonized worrying that I would get typhoid fever, and they would chop my hair down to the scalp, like some children in the poor neighborhoods. And even after your hair was chopped, sometimes you died anyway, and there you were, in a beautiful white casket, bald."

The other fancy lady put a pale hand around the gate's iron bar. "You know, Angélica, I think I'll meet this bearish ice cream Turk: he's been coming around for a long time now, and I've never met him. Get a load of that rrrr rugged configuration. I bet he has quite an ice cream cone." She chuckled.

"*Por Dios*, María Pía," the other one said, "be reasonable, not an ice cream Turk, really. And what about Esteban; what if he comes back all of a sudden."

"He won't be back until Friday, and besides, that's why you better be on the lookout for any car rumblings. . . ."

"Ay, *Dios Mío*, María Pía, and what would you do if he calls you 'my little patriotic dove'?"

"Ayyy, *qué horror!*" They both held on to the gate's iron bars, giggling. Their voices got lost in the midst of the price-haggling and questions and explanations going on around the wagon. My forehead itched, my jaws ached, my eyelids hung heavy with dust, my ribs smarted from the harness, my legs felt like straw. Maybe everything would sell quickly, leaving the wagon light as a sparrow, then I could speed to the nearest eatery.

Two panting and smiling children came back with money. One promptly dropped his cone, but before I had a chance to gauge the distance, he picked it up and wiped its coat of dirt against his ragged sleeve. Once I was lucky, and a child dropped his ice cream close enough for my neck to stretch without moving the wagon—which would have made my master furious—and scoop it up. It was hell on the teeth at first, but a second later a happiness invaded my mouth, so tender and deep that the memory of it lingered. The kid never stopped bawling until after we left. Ever since, I've kept my eyes roaming around for a similar opportunity; one of these days I'd get lucky again.

Rats; one of the fancy ladies opened the gate and advanced toward us. This was a bad sign. All the customers and oglers got deferentially out of the way to let her go by. My master was in a hunch-shouldered posture, hands in front, telling a woman in ragged clothes that he couldn't lower any more the price of the frying pan she wanted. When he saw the fancy lady coming, my master straightened up to his tall self, took his hat off, threw it in the wagon, smoothed his curly hair, and advanced to greet her. Ice cream? he asked with flair. The ragged woman that wanted the frying pan left with teary eyes. My master gave the fancy lady a cone and flashed his good-teeth smile when she said, "Oh! violet flavor!" He bent politely to ask permission to continue selling his wares. Hopefully, the fancy lady would depart with her treat back to her long-as-a-train house.

Rats; the fancy lady stayed, her eyes pinned on my master. The children slouching against the wall and trees who hadn't bought ice cream kept their eyes pinned on the tip of the fancy lady's tongue, following its slow survey of the very subtlety of the purple dome's texture.

When the last customer and ogler left, my master proceeded to close the wagon with big movements that shook the lavish curls on top of his head.

"Are you really a Turk, I mean, are you from Turkey?" the fancy lady asked coyly, then sucked the bottom of the cone, maybe it had started to drip. This was not looking good. My shoulders and haunches ached to go on, my legs were about to buckle under. I heard the reassuring sound of the wagon doors snapping as they fit together.

"My people are from Lebanon, you know where that is? It's a

Mediterranean country, but when people from Lebanon come to this country, they call us Turks. I guess it's shorter." They laughed. This was looking worse; laughing was always a very bad sign. I wiggled my ears to fend off flies that wanted to get inside, undaunted by the hairs, and bite me in shady comfort. I heard the iron bar slide through the loops to secure the doors; this time it slid carefully at first, then faster, two or three times. The fancy lady chuckled. I bent one leg and raised my neck in a hopeful readiness, maybe I'd feel my master's weight on the metal step, he would settle between me and the wagon and we would be on our way.

"It's too hot here, my ice cream melted." The fancy lady smiled. "Could you bring me an ice cream cone to the game room, over there, at the corner of the garden?" She pointed it out with a very pale hand. "It's really fresh and comfy. I'll wait there. With a cool glass of *granadina.*" Her fancy child hadn't gotten any ice cream, but she was asking for double portions.

I didn't hear my master say anything. The fancy lady turned around and floated away from the wagon without looking back. Before she disappeared beyond the gate and some rose-lined path, she tilted down her cone and snapped it to drop her ice cream, but way too far from my muzzle. All the children who had been slouching against the wall and trees rushed to it. The fastest one picked up the mush and licked it as it ran down his fingers and his arm.

My master opened the wagon and jumped inside. A whiff of cologne and a rustle of clothes came my way. My head felt heavy and dropped down, my nostrils got dirt inside, I sneezed. With my neck down I lifted my dusty eyelids and looked at the road ahead, reverberating, but otherwise perfectly still, waiting, waiting for us to trot over it and get to the eatery.

Translated by Elena Castedo

A
Time of
Mourning

MARTHA
CERDA

Now I know that Joaquín was twenty years older than Sofía, an inequality that she softened under the downy lip of a small-town woman, with tortoiseshell combs on each side of her head and a generously ample apron. But back then it was difficult for me to guess Sofía's age, always behind the iron entry gate, receiving bread in the morning or watering the garden in the afternoon. Her husband, on the other hand, came and went in his car which was driven by a chauffeur who called him "Don Joaquín," upon opening the door with a bend of the waist that made his employer appear to be much taller than he really was. The car took Joaquín, leaving the carport open, which gave his wife an opportunity to secretively peek out into the street before closing it.

Sofía spoke only with the children. Among ourselves we remarked that she spoke by singing and that she ended her words with either "u" or "i," from which the adults determined the couples' place of origin: "So far as I'm concerned, they come from Michoacán," my mother said. "No, it's in Tepa where they speak like that," contradicted my father. "Except they look like the people in Uruapan, and if they make guava jelly, surely that's where they're from." I never learned how to differentiate between one place and another, just as I didn't know how to differentiate between a woman who was pregnant and one who wasn't. So I spent many years waiting for Sofía to have a child, and she never had one.

When they arrived, there were many of us children on the block. We all used to pass by the house on the corner to go to the store, but none got to know the new neighbors the way I did. First I became friends with the cat, which I picked up one day when he was lost. I asked at various homes if it was theirs, until the only house left was the one on the corner. I knocked with my nine years palpitating inside of me; Sofía opened the door. It was the first time she ever offered me cookies and tea. It was her cat, it couldn't have been anyone else's: black, completely black.

The mysteries about the couple began to disturb me when I found out that Joaquín had died. The wake was held with so much discretion that no one noticed Sofía's sadness, dressed as she always was. Nevertheless, behind her thick and long eyelashes hid a reserved cunning, the kind of Good Fridays, when we went to church only for the meatless pastries. Joaquín died precisely on Holy Thursday without altering that week's mourning. When Easter arrived, no one remembered him anymore: Sofía, like a reminiscence of herself, continued watering the garden, making guava jelly, and looking down the street from afar, under her thick eyebrows which accentuated her widowhood.

Sofía's house faced onto two streets and, from both, one could see her sitting behind a window, embroidering, knitting, attending to her memories, wrapped in a black robe.

The second time I entered her house, making my way through the flowerpots filled with ferns and the multicolored cages, I found her talking to the canaries. Her hands, extremely white, trembled under the yellowish wings of two chicks whose mother had died. She looked at me without releasing the birds and said: "Joaquín promised me that you would come sooner or later. Come in." Then she led me to the living room and served a boiling cup of tea which I drank in sips. Sitting in front of me, she observed me, lightly touching my skin with her look.

I went back the next morning, the next and the next, trapped by Sofía's long eyelashes or by the clamor of her hands, or by her way of saying things as if she were singing. Without protesting I helped her knit baby clothes, embroider, and prepare a basket for a baby. She, meanwhile, talked about her life with Joaquín, placing his picture below the erratic light given off by a candle that was reflected in Sofía's hair.

At first my house was three houses away from her, then two, then one, and finally I found myself looking through her gate. I didn't realize at what point I learned to differentiate between the herbs of fecundation and those of rejuvenation, but one evening I caught myself invoking the spirit of love and drinking out of Sofía's cup. I never thought she could go beyond making tea, lighting candles, and mixing herbs, but in time I realized that an unknown Sofía took hold of her and me in the waning hours of daylight. "Joaquín assured me that I would never be alone again," she exclaimed with conviction, and I repeated her words without remembering who had said them first, she or I.

One early morning I woke up thinking of Joaquín, as I might have known him long ago, before I was born: and it's because the night before I had dreamed about him, he was calling me "Joaquín." I explained to him that I wasn't him, he was mistaken. Without recognizing me, he kept calling me "Joaquín." When I told Sofía about it, she wasn't surprised: I had an identical dream, she said, and then we both started humming the same song with no forethought. From that day on, if she gets hurt, I feel it: if I'm hungry, Sofía eats and I am satisfied. Nor can we keep anything from each other, I know that Sofía awaits the new moon, which is the day I'll turn fifteen, to carry out her plan: Each nightfall she practices her nuptials all alone, laying naked her widowhood little by little; then her flesh is filled with diminutive tongues that cover her from head to toe.

Today we woke up singing, certain that Sofía will not bleed for nine months when, with her own hand, she will cut our baby's umbilical cord. At twilight, as I straightened out the bird's cage where the female laid her eggs, I began to desire her. We went to the bedroom, closed the windows, and turned off the lights. The edges of the night clung to her mouth, darkening it. Nocturnal words, kept silent by day, awoke the silence, filling it with suggestions, with demands, with anxiousness. Sofía opened her body to desire, taking off her clothes and covering up with illusions and making the new moon grow in me, until our arms and legs were united in one sole desire: Sofía's, and she feverishly pronounced Joaquín's name with more and more vehemence. Just like in the dream, I screamed to her that I wasn't him, that she was mistaken. Sofía seemed not to hear me; at last, she proclaimed: "It has to be this way."

In front of Joaquín's picture we loved and hated each other at the same time and all my pent-up forces exploded with fury in her womb.

Now I know that Sofía is twenty years older than I; that under her apron her skin is infinite, and from now on we will always share the same sorrow: Sofía thinks of Joaquín: I, of her.

Translated by Sylvia Jiménez-Andersen

Even if I Bathed in the Purest Waters

For Juan Balbontín

DIAMELA
ELTIT

Beyond the horizon, it extends and proliferates. The burlap earth that brings the worst omens. The goat herders are distressed by their herds' poor stamina. The men, women, and children from the neighboring towns make frequent pilgrimages with growing numbers of offerings. The soldiers, quartered, prepare their weapons because they expect a massive uprising destined to challenge the taxes which, they claim, have been raised to the point of being unreachable. Conspiracy has already become an inoffensive exercise, and it is now common to see murmuring groups of people gathered, without the slightest caution, on public street corners, in spite of the presence of known spies who don't know how to memorize the various seditious conversations. The drought further aggravates the dejection, harming the animals and ruining the crop harvests. Due to the lack of rain, the soil rises in dust and the pilgrims' bodies look like rows of ocherous ghosts lining the paths. The voices of the preachers, who brazenly announce a deathly future brought about by the abandonment of traditions, are heard everywhere. The names of the gods multiply, and it is no longer known what ancient vengeance drives them. The names of the gods multiply, and it is possible to see how the multitude of offerings accumulate on the altars. And beyond, in a moving and sterile union, the burlap earth desperately couples with the bush.

I stir. My body rises in the midst of a familiar harmony. (I move in this lacerating and almost frozen time which transpires solely for the benefit of the monotonous completion of a myth.) My arms, my feet, my hands, my hips, my shoulder. The roundness of my limbs is diminished. The eagerness in the gazes of those around me springs from the perfection of each of my gestures. Ah, today John's head will fall, John's head will again roll. Over fifty years have gone by since the moment of the event and we are still chained to the same infinite scene. John and I. But John remains distant, drunk at the tavern. I know. When all is said and done, prior to and beyond my presence, when my dance is ended, John's head will be decapitated.

Oh my mother, my mother, my mother. After more than fifty years I can still smell my mother's body. Today I see and smell my mother's body. I sniff the tormented and beautiful contour of my mother, who talks to herself underneath the veils as an insult to her days' useless flight. My mother, wrapped in veils, weeps. Her husband quickly makes his way through every nook and cranny, searching for her, for us. My stepfather violently opens the heavy doors of the rooms with an incredible fury. But my mother, obstinate, hasn't yet made up her mind to surrender me. A few days ago I celebrated my fourteenth birthday. I am already fourteen and my mother, between sobs, tells me to go to the main hall, where the zither waits for me. And John, submerged in the tavern, still doesn't understand that beyond his desire, was mine, my desire.

"You laughed," John said to me.

"No," I answered.

"Yes," he insisted, "you laughed."

There was a night of dancing to honor the innumerable powerful guests who awaited the aesthetic and cautious fall of each of my veils. Yes, I dance throughout this night, with my stepfather as the guest of honor. In my mind I once again dance all night.

(Outside, the soldiers remain, along with the midgets, the traitor, and the small provincial court's jester.)

Ah, during a night of dancing, over fifty years ago, I defeated Sala, Elam, Azeir, Arafaxad, Peleq, Joctan. Meanwhile, John, very pale, drunk in a secret corner, away from that unstable recital, spoke of innocence and mentioned Salif, Ofir, Jabab, Almodad, Cus, Misraim, Misraim, Misraim. How could I have understood then that John was looking for a god in the slums, that he had already lost his head?

My mother, my mother, my mother. My mother, protected by the veils, laments the injury. Her dark hair, smeared with oil, falls over her bed's delicate pillows. My stepfather, who is also my blood relative, desolately wanders the halls possessed by an indescribable guilt. I approach my mother to stroke her hair and she clings to my neck and praises my purity with wavering words. I smell my mother's entangled hair and I lean over and console her. My stepfather has arrived. He looks at us, looks at me. My stepfather stops and waits for an answer. My mother looks at him with contempt and then, with an imperceptible motion, covers my torso with a veil.

My stepfather is afraid of my mother. I know that fear. My stepfather needs my mother today, but she refuses him. Hidden behind the curtains, I observe them, for my mother has asked me to guard her. The obligation of witnessing this farce, which I know too well, disgusts me. I first saw John, who was the object of so much talk, in the early morning hours. My stepfather's favorite was just as people said, a peasant from the quarries, a yokel exiled from the stone work. I looked intently at my stepfather's chosen one, without being able to hide my disappointment, while he feigned ignorance of my presence, demonstrating that overtly ostentatious aloofness that I've gotten from certain seditious underlings with whom my stepfather likes to surround himself. Without abandoning my uneasiness, I approached the luminous locust tree against which he leaned:

"So you are John," I said, "my stepfather's favorite."

"Yes," he answered, "I am John, the one destined to guard your uncle's honesty."

I am over sixty years old and the dance still haunts me. My mother's smell is in me, it follows me.

(While the soldiers, the midgets, the traitor, and the provincial court's jester still roam interminably outside; they follow me.)

I am over sixty years old and I dance and dance and dance. John's neck was always suitable to its perfect cicatrix. An incomprehensible God lied when He said I would be bone of one bone, flesh of one flesh. My bones belong only to me, my flesh is still not joined except to the dance. John will be there, alone in the tavern, his head bent, thinking it possible that one day He will inhabit the earth.

"Nude. You were nude," John said.

Then silence came, and after the silence his usual, and already much written about, litany.

He said (to me):

"For ever and ever, if you are on the left, I will go to the right. If you are on the right, I will go to the left."

"Fine," I answered, "if that is what you prefer."

My mother possesses a timelessness that was given her as a gift through the ambiguous generosity of the gods. My mother is as girlish as myself, even more so. My stepfather and I must comfort her almost every morning, when she awakens trembling in sobs. My mother is horrified by her corruption and, to soothe herself, she must resort to an interminable set of baths; yes, she requires oil, or herbal, or goat's-milk baths to ease the stigmas that haunt her in her turbulent dreams.

And I prepare her bath with manic prolixity, sorting, with my own hands, the vital herbs, careful that the milk retain its freshness, and making sure that the oil is solely from the finest crops and that everything be smooth and warm so that it may bring her body the appeasement it needs. My mother's baths could take hours and even days, and I am the only one who may replace the liquids so that they will not, even for a moment, lose their warmth. My mother shields her nakedness from foreign gazes, for she knows that her perfection could produce turbid desires in the eyes of those who glance at her body. She senses that in unfulfilled desire there lies an enemy possessed by an atrocious humiliation. A humiliation as powerful and incisive as desire itself. My mother wants to thus avoid falling into the ring of terror inspired by her certainty that someone is preparing an ambush. I painstakingly guard my mother's baths, and I make sure that nobody can see us as I let the oil fall over her head. Once she feels that she has recovered her strength, she thanks me, stroking my face, and she forgets the previous night's deadly dreams. Afterward, with light steps, she goes to her room. If the liquid is still warm, I disrobe and submerge myself in the waters that have cured my mother's body, and I wait. I wait.

I saw John leaning against the sturdy wood of the locust tree. He was surrounded by a servile group of people, among which I recognized a few individuals given to espionage and murmurings. (In the madness of time, more than fifty years have passed since that meeting.) I had been informed that John had my stepfather's blessing. He seemed captivated by the young man's sharp tongue, which had the ability to turn answers into questions and affirmations into bewilderment. My stepfather submitted John to extensive rhetorical bouts in which flowed the most profound ideas that time and history had accumulated. One particularly memorable digression regarding origins lasted an entire night, during which my stepfather questioned John about fire, the heavens, the light, and the changing of the seasons. It appeared to be that my stepfather, exhausted, conceded to John's obstinacy, and then, troubled by various anxieties, was, for three nights, unable to sleep. Yet, when I approached the locust tree I was immediately irritated by John's imposture, that arrogance masked by an intolerable neutrality.

"So you're John," I said.

"So you're John," I said, "my stepfather's favorite."

"Yes, I'm John," he answered, "the one destined to guard your uncle's honesty."

"You've chosen quite a useless occupation," I told him. "Why don't you pay attention to your own integrity?"

The pace of the day, with its nocturnal conversion, tires me. Far from the large cities, all opulence seems destined to failure. My mother assures me that in the large cities one lives lavishly with a plentitude of knowledge we will never encounter. She objects to the simplicity of the province we reside in, and refuses to learn the dialects used by the oppressed peoples around us. But I know she is familiar with most of these dialects and can decipher the most intricate conversations. My mother speaks more than ten languages, thanks to an amazing ability that lets her master foreign words. But she'd rather forget her learning so as to avoid making my stepfather uneasy, lest it awaken bad omens in him. I've heard my mother sing beautiful songs in more than ten languages when an unexpected joy overcomes her and, on those occasions, my ear falls in love with the prodigious cadence of her voice. My mother asserts that her sorrows and mine are produced by the country's monotonous sleepiness and that we are captives to its nature like a slave is to the rock. My mother, as an emblem of protest against the nuisance that our fate has handed us, has confessed that she is planning to shave her head. At that moment John's image must have superimposed itself on her words, because my mother's hair, as we all know, is sacred. Possessed by a terrible grief, I now walk toward the main hall to face the zither, the harp, and my body's premature duty.

My stepfather has called for a day of fasting to invoke the gods' compassion. Self-serving propaganda turns the fasting not into a ceremony for repentance, but rather into an occasion for vanity and fun. My mother is upset at my stepfather's making that decision without consulting her, ruining the peace she had maintained throughout the day. She refuses to leave her room, and has twice rejected my company. Deprived of her affection, I wander through the rooms, heartbroken, among obsequious assistants whose words seem banal. My stepfather does not visit my mother today and seems absorbed and pleased by the image of a wealthy merchant's young daughter who showed up perfumed with strong incense. Although I am close to my stepfather, he refuses to heed my displeasure. I go to the main hall and find solace in the harp. Its sound fills me with piety and sweetness, but my stepfather sends a messenger ordering me to stop immediately. I must abandon the harp. I walk through the corridors pierced by a pernicious heat. I am fourteen years old. I am sickened.

I am over sixty years old. My room is filled with mirrors that are placed here to confirm my presence. I wouldn't know how to recognize myself outside of them, for I live only in the reflections projected by their glass. My body returns to me in the mirrors as the most prominent sign of a broken existence. Do I exist in spite of this? Do we exist? I ask myself. The chaos has already been eternally consumed, but my nostalgia still claims it. I dance and dance in front of the mirror. Although I made myself terribly vulnerable, I have not died yet and neither has John. He will be speaking at the taverns, as if possessed, invoking the name of a father who turned out to be insensible when he scorned the splendor of his own son's name. Ah, John, digressing in the tavern while I am reduced to this crude flash in the mirrors. But it is entirely inevitable. I know. I know. Yes, today John's head will again roll at the instant that my body's final movement is complete, and the only image remaining in my sight will be the memory of his prophetic and malignant smile.

"Ah," I said to John, "abandon your dark words with which you hope to denounce the shame and wickedness that, according to you, you've come to set straight."

That afternoon I found myself in a state of confusion, not knowing to whom or to what unknown cause I was obligated to surrender my soul. Out of my confusion I secretly turned to John, knowing I was treading the dangerous terrain of prohibitions. We had met in the room in which he had enclosed himself to purge his former sins and of that meeting the only witness is my own memory. But it happened. It happened.

"Your mother is the one responsible," he told me.

"How could you lie with such impunity? My stepfather is the one responsible," I said.

"Be done with your pointless judgments. You have come looking for me to corrupt my judgment."

"No," I told him, "don't add to the deception. It is you who have come here expecting me to transport you to a glory that seems brutal to me. Because your arrogance knows no bounds, you have reached us guided by a fanatical impulse."

That was how it began. And there were the straw mattress, the walls, a basin filled with water, the image of my mother impacted in my brain, and my body driven crazy with need. After that evening, during which all miracles were denied us, John sought refuge in the unconditional allegory of wine.

This darkened sky, it is as if the sand, threatening and anarchic, had dispersed itself, mad with fury, toward the heavens. The pilgrims advance with a dramatic slowness through the dust storms, shielding their offerings between their clothing. The drought leaves a trail of terrible waste, which increases the emptiness of the landscape and makes even more hostile the bodies of the marchers. The children who accompany the caravans maintain an expression of stupor in their eyes while resisting, with an incomprehensible loyalty, the sands' blows, protecting their faces with the rough cloths that cover them. Why recount the number of animals left dead along the roads or reproduce the agonizing death rattles? The temple is visible in the distance, due to its unique architecture, sterile in the face of such misery. The gods maintain their eyes closed in their temple, confused in the state between sleep and vigil. The addiction to the slumbering gods lies in the omnipotence of their silent desires. The rock is not made whiter by this dust storm, and the quarries still cannot resist the blows that crumble the rock. John, the most composed of the laborers in the last quarry, gently leans and listens to his own voice, which proclaims with an almost divine perfection: "Soon death will hold you in its arms."

Translated by Delia Poey

Amalia

So he drove out the man;
and he placed a Cherubim at
the East of the Garden
of Eden; and a flaming sword
which turned every way, to
keep the way of the tree of life.

GENESIS 3:24

ROSARIO
FERRÉ

At last I am inside the forbidden garden and I can be myself, knowing that this is going to be all the way and to no avail. This time I'm going through with this to the very end, where there will be neither quenching nor stopping, hemming in by drying sheets buffeted by the wind and screaming gulls that excrete salt droppings all around me. I begin to rock in my arms this melting bundle which used to be you, Amalia, as well as I, together we were one inseparable being, waiting for the day when we could finally enter the garden, knowing that one day they'd finally leave open the door. Now everyone has left; the house is smoldering like a bleached bone and I can sigh with relief because I've finally begun to perspire, because at last I can perspire all I want.

One of the maids found me with my eyes shut lying on the ground like a rag doll. And she began to scream and I could hear her screaming next to me though I was far away, and then I felt them lift me carefully from the ground and carry me to my room where they put me to bed before running to find Mother to tell her about it. Now my right arm is heavy like a log and I feel the needle in it, and although my eyes are shut I know it's the needle because I've felt it before and I know I must be patient and that I can't move, because if I move it'll hurt even more. I can hear the maids crying behind the door and I hear Mother nearby, yes, Doctor, it hadn't been ten minutes before they found her lying on the ground in the garden, she ran away from the maids when they were doing the laundry in the nearby sink, that's what they're here for, just to take care of her, but she's slier than a squirrel and she slips past them all the time; as soon as their attention is distracted by something she flies out into the sunlight like a moth; she hides under the elephant ears of the arum leaves and spies on them, looking for a chance to scuttle out to the garden where the sheets are hung out to dry, and after making sure nobody's around she lies down on the floor like a common slut, burning under the sun and dirtying her white dress, her white socks, her white shoes, with her little-girl's face upturned to the sky and her arms opened wide, because she wants to know what happens, she says, she wants to know what it's like. I can't even sleep anymore, Doctor, it's the fourth time it's happened and the next time we'll find her dead; the worst part is not knowing how to treat it, the illness doesn't even have a name, seeing her onion-white skin shrivel and turn transparent at the least ray of sunlight, seeing her sweating through every pore as if she were a sponge and not an eleven-year-old girl and someone were squeezing her. At night I dream I see her lying on the turf all dried up and wrinkled, her head too big for her body and her skin bloated and purple, sticking to the seed of her bones.

Then I hear the doctor ask me, were there any bloodlines between your family and your husband's; not that I know of, we weren't related at all if that's what you mean, not even distant cousins, why are you asking me that; maybe I'm wrong but in cases like these the cause of genetic degeneration may have been incest. Incest, what do you mean, Doctor, you must be out of your mind; it's reasonably common in Puerto Rican families, it happens in ten percent of them. And then I hear my mother slam the door angrily after her and go out of the room, while the maids go on whispering on the other side of the wall and I hear the doctor give them strict instructions to make me rest and stay in bed, keeping me from going out again in the sun. Then he shuts the door softly behind him and leaves.

Mother brought my uncle in to see me that afternoon. He was wearing his military uniform, starched and ironed like an archangel's, with the golden eagle gleaming over the patent-leather visor of his cap. He was carrying a large pink box under his right arm and kept his left arm draped over mother's bare shoulders. I can still see them standing close together at the foot of my bed, looking as if they were melting because the drops of perspiration kept spilling down my face and running into my eyes and they made the whole world look like it was shimmering underwater, mother's delicate features becoming alternately narrower and wider, her brother's features an almost exact replica of her own, going from concave to convex, from longer to shorter, one dark-haired and the other blond, one dressed like a woman and the other like a man, animatedly sharing the same gestures, exchanging the same masques between them as if they were bouncing tennis balls with mortal precision, an even match since birth with the advantage of love to their score. They talk to me but I know they're using me as a sounding board to talk among themselves, I'm just a whitewashed wall to bounce off tennis balls; standing together at the foot of my bed, they use me to communicate. I've brought you a present today, says my uncle, and he opened the box and brought out a beautiful doll bride carefully wrapped in rustling silk paper; it's a very fine doll, he said, it's not like the ones that are made today, and he began to wind the small bronze butterfly on your back so that you began to flutter a dainty mother-of-pearl fan in your hand and a tune of dancing silver pins began to tinkle inside your chest. Then my uncle laughed as if he were enjoying a private joke of some kind and I felt as if a stream of white tennis balls bounced all over me. After they had gone out I laid you by my side on the bed and I wondered at what my uncle had meant. You were, as he had pointed out, a very singular doll, but you had one defect; you were made of wax.

Poor Amalia, now your face is melting and one can almost see the delicate wire net on which your features were molded; your face makes me think of the eye of a huge fly. I try to protect you with my body but it's no good; the sun comes from everywhere and bounces off the walls and hits you on the rebound; it comes from above, from the starched white sheets, from the burnt ground. Now your lids have melted and you look at me with wide-open eyes, like those fish in subterranean lakes that need no lids because there is no sun and no one ever knows if they are asleep or awake. Now your mouth has melted and I feel angry at the other dolls because they were to blame;

they made Gabriel a slave to their whims when their destiny was to keep to their own ground, living in their own quarters which gave unto the balconied galleries where they were to act out their predestined lives, caring for the tea tables and the flowered vases, the china and the matching table linen, being gracious hostesses to the colonels, the ambassadors, and the foreign ministers. But they didn't want to; they simply refused to accept their lot. Now the perspiration is running into my eyes again and they are starting to burn, but I can still see Mother standing at the foot of the bed smiling down at me, although try as I may I can only see my uncle in fragments, exactly as I saw him a while ago when I looked in the dining room window.

On the day Mother died I took off Amalia's wedding dress and dressed her in mourning weeds. As my father had died many years before, my uncle came to live in our house with Gabriel, his chauffeur. A few days after moving in, he threw out Mother's old servants and took in three young girls to do the housework, María, Adela, and Leonor. They were very pretty and he treated them kindly, almost as if they weren't maids at all; he was always sending them to the beauty parlor and giving them all kinds of trinkets and cheap perfume, and he assigned each of them a different bedroom in the house. Although the girls were grateful to my uncle and were always very cordial to him, it was clear they were crazy about Gabriel from the start. When Gabriel sat at the kitchen table to sing after dinner was over, dressed in his ink-blue chauffeur's uniform which blended in so well with the color of his skin, his eyes would gleam in a special way, and his tone was so strong it sounded as if a whole chorus were chanting in his chest. In the evening he was always singing; he'd lick the white-tiled walls of the kitchen with his tar-thick voice; he'd melt it over the gas flame before winding it inside his mouth once again. And all the time wearing his cap on his head and the girls serving him coffee at the kitchen table. Then he'd start to play on the chopping board as if it were a drum, one two three, take it off, cut the knuckle of the pig, four five six, take it off, carve the hoof of the bull, seven eight nine, take it off, wring the neck of the geese, and the girls would leave off what they were doing and they'd begin to follow him around the kitchen in a dancing queue; they know they shouldn't do it but they couldn't help themselves; they couldn't resist the music, keeping the beat with knives and forks against the stove, one two three, shibam-shibam, hitting the saucer, the tureen, the cup, four five six, shibam-shibam, shoveling the ladle, the scoop, the spoon, shibamshibam, cleaning the inside of the swordfish and the kingfish, shibamshibam, mashing their marrow for lentil soup, shibamshibam, dancing on their toes and playing on their knives as if they were xylophones, shibamshibam. The truth is I used to hide behind the kitchen door and spy on them as all this was going on, following the beat with the tip of my white polished shoe, until the day Gabriel saw me and taking me by the wrists whisked me up in his arms and made me join in the dance. From that day onward, when Gabriel wasn't driving my uncle's car, he'd be dancing and singing with us all the time.

My uncle had never married, as he had devoted himself heart and soul to his military career. I never liked him, and even before Mother died, I had always avoided being near him. He always went out of his way to be nice to me. He had ordered the maids to follow the doctor's orders and keep me from going out of the house into the garden, but to leave me in complete liberty inside. In the following months he gave me several more dolls to play with, pink roly-poly ones which I baptized María, Adela, and Leonor.

Not long after he came to live with us he was made general, and that was when the visits to the house of the ambassadors, the ministers, and the colonels began. As I used to play with my dolls in the dining room, half hidden behind the carved oak sideboard, I'd watch them going in and coming out of my uncle's office like an endless procession of archangels, always immaculate in their gold-braided uniforms and letting their hands fall on the green crystal knob of the door. I couldn't understand what they were talking about in there but I liked to listen when their voices rose in inspired cadences, almost as if they were praying in church.

When these visits began our games in the kitchen had to stop. At the end of each visit my uncle would take his guests into the living room where he would make María, Adela, and Leonor serve them drinks and snacks. Then they would all sit around and chatter and make friends; since many of them were foreigners my uncle thought it was a good idea that they get to know us better, that we should show them that we have pretty girls who know how to frost their hair, wear nice clothes, and make interesting conversation. And of course the girls loved it; they laughed at the jokes and after a few drinks climbed on the furniture to show off their underwear or to have a Miss Universe contest, drinking from their silk pumps as if they were champagne glasses and after a while taking off their clothes when the visitors insisted that the room had become too hot.

At first I used to listen to the din from behind the door and I felt rather sorry for them until the day the girls came to my room and took me into the living room. There they brushed my long brown curls and stood me under the crystal chandelier with my starched dress very crisp and spry, which made them think of a white butterfly. Then they lifted me up and sat me on my uncle's knees, filling my hands with mint pasties and smiling at me all the while, because they so wanted to please him. From that day onward, every time I heard someone knocking at the door of the house I'd run to open it myself, and I'd take the visitor by the hand to lead him to where all the frolicking was going on. When they stared at me as though they couldn't believe what they saw, I'd simply shake my brown curls and white silk bow so they wouldn't be misled, and I'd walk on tiptoe down the hallway pulling them along until we reached the living room, where everybody was assembled.

As Gabriel and I had nothing to do in the house during these meetings, we'd spend the day playing with my dolls. We had turned the old sideboard into their summer palace, and we'd let them air themselves, walking them down the balustered galleries where Mother's French porcelain dishes were displayed. We took the dolls out of their boxes and as the sideboard was very tall and elaborate, we assigned each one a different floor. Then we established a rule; in each floor the lodger could do as she wished, but she could under no circumstances visit the other floors, or else she'd have to face a death sentence. After thus establishing the rules of our game, Gabriel and I spent some very amusing afternoons with my dolls, until the day he said he wanted to go back to the girls in the kitchen, because he preferred to sing and dance with them instead.

That day I had become very angry because Gabriel had dared to take Amalia out of her box and had wanted to play with her; I don't want you to, don't touch her, I said, leave her alone, but he was much stronger than I; he began to rock her in his arms, singing to her all the time under his breath, until Amalia, oh oh oh, began to lose control of herself; she began to break the laws of the game, oh oh oh, she ran up and down the galleries lifting and lowering her skirts, oh oh oh, as if she had lost her mind, shaking the skirt's black silk folds between the balconies' banisters, oh oh oh, laughing for the first time with her tiny teeth shibamshibam, stepping on the garlic and onion with her bare heels, shibamshibam, oh oh oh, Mother, how I like the smell of scrub, the scrub of rub, oh oh oh, and then fleeing, Amalia running and screaming like a she-devil, like a dervished shrew, tripping on your skirts and rising again without caring about anything, because now you knew the price you'd have to pay. In the afternoons that followed, Gabriel and I went on playing with my dolls in the dining room, but our games were never the same. From then on Amalia could come and go through all the sideboard's galleries as freely as she wished.

Everything would have continued in the same way and we

would all have gone on feeling content in our own peculiar way, if it hadn't been for you, Amalia, because I got it into my head that you were feeling unhappy. My uncle had insisted that when I turned twelve years old I should make my First Communion. A few days before that date finally came about he asked me what I wanted as a present and I could only think of you, Amalia, of the many months you had spent in mourning and of how much you'd probably like to dress all in white once again. After all, you had been a bride to begin with, and for that reason your head had a delicate hidden spot on it, where a steel pin could be inserted to keep your orange-blossomed veil in place. But the rest of the dolls felt envious of you and so they were glad when they saw you become his slave, always going up and down the galleries; María, how much did you earn today, my uncle needs the money; Adela, remember that you owe me a white silk bow and a pair of stockings; Leonor, if you go on pretending you are ill, they'll kick you out of here and you can't risk it, not with your tint-burned hair and your chipped-china doll's face, and so they went on and on as you went in and out of their rooms with the pockets of your black skirt stuffed full of dollar bills mashed into balls.

I'd like a bridegroom for Amalia, I said defiantly, and he smiled as if he had expected my answer all the time. This morning he gave me the box just before going out, on our way to church. I was already wearing my gloves and was holding the candle in my hand, but I couldn't wait until we came back home. I started to open it right away and when I lifted the lid my heart just stopped beating. Inside there was a large blond doll dressed in gala white military uniform, all aglimmer with sparkling stripes and gold braid that fell plaited over his shoulders, and with the general's eagle glowing over the visor of his cap. I put the lid back on and struggled to hide my terror, picking up my candle, my rosary, and my First Communion missal with the host and chalice painted on the cover, as if nothing had happened. We went out into the street and my uncle, who was walking beside me, immediately opened his black umbrella over my head to keep away the sun. The church was nearby, and as we walked to it we formed a small cortege, my uncle and I at the head, María, Leonor, and Adela after us, and Gabriel silently bringing up the rear. I had completely forgotten about the military doll, which I had left unguarded inside its box, on top of the dining room table.

When we returned home we went into the garden, where my uncle had ordered we should have a small party in my honor. We sat on a bench, under the umbrella he held over my head, as the girls went to get the refreshments from the house. And then he began to talk to me in a patronizing way, sighing out the words like he was blowing out candles, and I realized that for years I had been expecting his speech, that I had known by heart what his words would be. He put his arm around my shoulders as he went on talking, and even though the droning in my ears wouldn't let me recognize the exact words, I understood perfectly what he was trying to say. It was then that I began to understand how Mother must have felt. As he talked, I kept my head bent and refused to look into his eyes, and this began to infuriate him more and more, because Mother always looked at him attentively when he spoke to her, although perhaps she only looked like that at him to defy him, but I couldn't look at him because I knew he was a coward, in spite of the medals, the braids, and the eagle shining in his cap, and one should never look cowards in the eye. When he saw I wouldn't look at him, he took away his umbrella so that the sun's rays would come at me from every side, and he put his hand over my small left breast. I sat there without moving for a few minutes, until I finally looked at him with all the hate I was capable of.

I certainly didn't expect what happened next, Amalia; it must have all been planned by the dolls living on the sideboard or perhaps it was all your doing, yes, now that I think of it that seems more probable, because after Gabriel sang to you for the first time you became daring and shameless, you felt you were free and could do whatever you pleased. The other dolls had gained weight and spent their lives leaning on the sideboard railings, looking out contentedly on the world and feeling their conscience was clear because they always did as they were told. They were, after all, just common plastic dolls made in Taiwan, with watered-down urine, nylon hair, and battery-powered voices. You tried all you could to make them rebel against him, reminding them again and again of their despicable state, living in apartments with pink porcelain bathtubs and tulip-shaped washbasins made in all colors, with closets bursting with clothes and jewelry and furs which they would caress at night when they got out of bed because they couldn't sleep. You didn't know that it was useless, that you were doomed to failure from the start because you belonged to another world and to another age, that your fine wax body had absolutely no practical use, that the delicate music box in your chest would soon become rusted and would one day burst in a tiny firework of chimes. And even if you knew you probably would still have gone on with your plan, acting with deliberation for a valid cause. You took the military doll out of his box, you stripped it of its insignias and medals and took off its white uniform; then you painted it all black, with the deepest blue tar you could find; you dyed its hair with blackberry juice, you stained its eyes with cobalt dust, and drew its lips with indigo blue. Then you dressed it in a chauffeur's uniform and placed a cap just like Gabriel's on its head. It was then that María, Adela, and Leonor came upon you, as they came up from the garden to bring the refreshments for the party, and they found you lying in the box, embracing each other tightly.

When my uncle heard the girls laughing and shrieking, he got up from the garden bench and went running into the house. I stayed where I was sitting, looking at the stains of perspiration that kept spreading slowly over my dress so that I hardly noticed when he came back holding you with both hands and shaking you violently; this is your doing, you little devil, you may look like your mother with that innocent look on your face but deep down you're just like the rest, I've given you everything you have and this is how you pay me back, you little slut, you may keep your nigger if you want him so badly; here's your doll to keep you company; now both of you can stay in the garden until you find out what's good for you. And then he threw you on my lap and slammed the door of the house after him, locking it from the inside.

It was sometime later, when there was already a pool of perspiration on the bench, that I began to hear strange noises coming from the house, one two three, shibamshibam, six, five, four, take it off. I dragged myself slowly to the dining room window and making an effort managed to pull myself over the sill so that I could look in. Gabriel was at the head of the queue, slicing off the chest, the arms, the hands with the kitchen knife flashing like a thunderbolt, exploding vases and centerpieces like empty heads against the walls, splitting open the furniture until its insides were spilled all over the floor, splintering the mirrors like silver skins, shattering the wineglasses on the polished mahogany floors, bursting exploding detonating until the whole world seemed to be flying apart at the seams. And behind him came the girls, dancing and screaming at the same time, setting fire to the tapestries and to the rugs; they've put out his eyes and they are pouring them in a glass, taking out all the fine clothes from the closets and throwing them out the window; they've cut off his hands and they've served them to him on a platter, tearing the silk curtains from the windows and slashing the bedcovers into shreds; they've opened his mouth wide open and they've stuck something pink and long in it that I can't recognize, singing all the while one two three, shibamshibam, four five six, take it off, as they dance around the dining room floor. My face stares back at me calmly from the windowpane, lit up by the flushed light of the flames. Then the glass shatters and my face shatters and the smoke begins to stifle me and I see Gabriel standing beyond the open window, blocking my way with his sword.

When the fire began to die out I sat there quietly, as the last rays of the afternoon sun bounced back from the walls of the house. Then I walked slowly to the middle of the garden and took Amalia in my arms and began to rock her. I rocked you for a long time, trying to protect you from the heat with my own body as you slowly began to melt. Then I placed you on the ground and lay down next to you, carefully stretching out my legs so that my white skirt my white socks my white shoes wouldn't get dirty and now I turn my face up to the sky and I feel happy because I'm finally going to know what happens; I'm finally going to learn what it's like.

Translated by Rosario Ferré

A Script for Every House

MAGALI GARCÍA RAMIS

Voice-over: All the houses are eyes
that glow and lie waiting.

All the houses are mouths
that spit, bite, and kiss.
All the houses are arms
pushing and drawing one closer.
Gusts of shadows and jungles
creep forth from every house.
Insatiated blood wails in each house.
In unison, all the houses scream
assail and ravage each other.
In unison, they all calm down
become fertile, and wait.

—Miguel Hernández

(When the poem ends, the lights on the set will be turned up to reveal a living room in a suburban house. It'll be the afternoon. The camera will slowly approach a woman and a man sitting on a sofa, as it moves in for a clasp, the woman closes a book.)

I'm telling you that everything will have to start on a greenish day. On that day, at the same time, four cars will approach a housing development. Each of the four drivers will be the new owner of a new house, on block K, in Villa Atenas. On that greenish day, each one will get to know a newly finished house, to begin to live in a recently built house. The houses will be identical: cubes, with a single carport on the right and a door and a glass window on the left; they'll be painted an identical white and all will have identical new walls, without any thoughts or human emotions resonating from them—unless they remember the sexual fantasies of the union painter who remained turned on during the entire job by the pictures of the naked women on the Amigo hardware store calendar. Each will enter his house and slowly their dreams will mesh with the air, above, inside, and under the houses. Each of the houses.

(*Panoramic shot of the bedroom so we can see every piece of furniture, every painting, every detail. Afterward the camera pans back to the woman.*)

A woman will enter K-5, a woman filled with many fears, which you'll discover little by little. In her youth she was beautiful and had many suitors, you should understand that. Now she's fat and feels an inordinate repugnance toward lizards. Seeing them gives her a horrible fright because they creep sinuously; and the fear she feels is so immense that she almost faints when she sees them. Fine, yes, go ahead, whisper that she's a "frustrated old maid," a frustrated spinster, as if that noun and its eternal adjective could explain that she's a woman who has known how to feel and love, a woman capable of giving herself. She, the one from K-5, do you know what she did that day? She had to ask her brother for $10 for gas to be able to get to her new house because the last $14.97 from her salary slipped through her fingers for mustache-removal depilatory cream. God damn it, don't laugh! Mustache-removal cream! Because in Fomento, the Office of Economic Development, all the women go to work stylishly dressed and well-groomed.

·   ·   ·

They spend their salaries on their bodies, on their hair, on their complexion, on their clothes, and she was (is?) more attractive and more of a somebody than any of them—skin-bleached-black-women and exiled-Cuban-whores! She'll be a decent woman, from a good family, a graduate from the exclusive Las Madres School, and . . . everyone will feel sorry for her. Yes, that's what I said, sorry!

The first thing she'll hang on the walls of her house, to make it her home, will be a pair of retouched photos, in oval wooden frames, of her father and mother, both now dead, may they rest in peace.

A newlywed couple will enter K-7, a couple wanting to believe that the world is as big as the love they share, and as spotless as their new K-7 home. They want to believe it, but they know better. He came back from Vietnam and still trembles each night in his sleep. He wants to escape all his haunting memories and he snuggles up next to her to silence the screams in his nightmares, screams louder than cannon fire, cries of terror from little children, their faces melting, in a hellhole of a town where they threw napalm, and then the man from K-7 appears in the dream, and the children run and they are caught in a photo, and they become famous, naked, burnt children, captured by a journalist with his camera, in a picture that goes around the world, in the same way that everything comes around again to the young man in K-7 when he smells fried ripe plantains, because Vietnam looks so much like Puerto Rico, and he sees children running in front of a hut where people are frying ripe plantains, and the delicious contagious smell mingles with the smell of burning flesh of small children and he is never again able to separate them.

· · ·

(The camera follows the man, who gets up from the sofa, rubs his neck, and sits down again, now on the floor at the foot of the sofa.)

She received him at the National Guard airport, his soul torn to pieces, and she took him, with his Afro, with his vile speech like that of a man lacking religion, and his unsatisfied longing to make love to her, directly to the CREA Home for drug detoxification; and she supported him there for the two years the treatment lasted, visiting him each month and praying for him at the temple next to her house, yes, the one in San Juan they want to close because people say it's too noisy. She went on like that until he was returned to her rehabilitated and well-groomed. She's gentle and sweet and she doesn't shave her legs which he fondles lovingly because they love each other, there won't be any doubt about that. The first thing she'll place on the wall will be a picture of the Divine Pastor with big, blue, faggot-like eyes and a lot of lambs around him and a little one nestled in his arms, painted with such skill that one can almost hear her bleating, "beeeh." The first thing he'll place in the house will be a wooden Indian chief, an encrusted mosaic that he made in the workshop of the CREA Home, a symbol that he can create. Everyone will instantly love these two.

A family will go into K-9, a family with four kids, two dogs, a canary, a pregnant hamster, and a small town past which they want to forget. The man of the house has just completed, with special distinction, a Dale Carnegie course, "How to Improve Your Business Personality," and in six months, thanks to that course, and to the godfather of one of his children, who's a Mason, he got a job with the phone company in the metropolitan area, but he still doesn't know many people there and he wants to make friends. His wife and faithful companion, only his second girlfriend, has given birth to four children whom he adores, although the oldest child, let's be fair, didn't turn out like him but inherited everything from the other side. Sickly and blue-eyed like his maternal grandfather, he spends all his time locked in his room reading instead of going out to have a good time and playing baseball like other kids his age. What's more, to top it all, in an act of defiance of his father, he's a pacifist and a little hippie. A "Pa-ci-fist" says the father since he received nonsolicited literature by mail from left-wing American organizations. But his wife, an obliging person and a good cook, an expert in the best remedies for drunkenness and chronic constipation, which he suffers from, gave him a Second Son —that one is worth a lot. At thirteen he plays dominoes like a Titan and soon they'll teach him to drive. He takes care of the animals and he loves them, and he won second prize with Brownie last year at the dog show at the Dorado Beach Hotel.

(Circular camera movement focusing on the two of them. The man reclines his head on the woman's legs. The light from the lamp to the right of the sofa creates a soft atmosphere now that the sun has set.)

Also there's the girl who at ten helps his wife in the house and manicures her nails and sews by herself—that's how it goes, like a neat and tidy young woman of the past, a true young lady, the apple of her daddy's eye—she sews her own little blue and gold skirt to join the cheerleading squad. And the last one, the pampered five-year-old —because God wanted it that way since they lost two in between— the Pampered One with the deep voice who's going to be a cop when he grows up to kill all the crooks, bang bang. The first thing the Mrs. will hang on the wall is the Last Supper, in relief, made of plaster that her in-laws gave them for their fifteenth wedding anniversary, and which takes up half of the dining room wall. The first thing the Mr. will hang on the wall will be a white and blue flag with a palm tree, and under it in Bodoni Bold lettering: THE NEW PROGRESSIVE PARTY, PUERTO RICO: THE 51ST STATE, WE'LL WIN AGAIN NEXT TIME. The first thing the Oldest Son will hang on the outside of his bedroom door, and later on the inside, because his father will threaten to kick down the door if he doesn't remove it from the outside, is a poster of the flag of the United States with a wounded dove flying over it and the word PEACE spelled out in bullet holes. The first thing the Second Son will hang on his bedroom wall will be a flag the same as his father's. The first thing the Beloved Daughter will hang on her closet wall will be a full-color poster of the exiled Cuban television star Rolando Barral with a bandanna tied around his neck. And the first thing the Pampered One will put on the wall of the K-9 bedroom he shares with the Second One will be all the fingerprints from his tiny fingers smeared with ice-cream from Mr. Ice who will go by every day at the same time playing a waltz to attract the children. The people from K-9 will have to be received with joy.

(*Shooting the upper halves of both. The man gets up, goes to the kitchen and brings back two glasses of whiskey and water. The woman takes a sip from hers.*)

A man in his forties will go into K-11 along with his *Doña*, who receives massages from the spirits, and his niece, who is also his godchild and is a public school teacher. He will have done terrible things in his youth, things one can't relate without giving them undue emphasis. What? You don't like what I'm saying? Come on, sit down, calm down, I'll say it hastily: he was poor; he ran in the streets; he kicked the canes from under lame people; he stole money from the offering box located in front of Our Lady of Providence at the Cathedral in San Juan; he peeked at his older sister when she was taking a bath and . . . no, don't get like that. All right . . . I'll talk about his wife, a *Doña*, a woman without much education, who every month buys herself new polyester pantsuits, and his niece, a woman with many ambitions in the political party, long sharp nails, and eyes the color of "I'll eat you up." The man never wanted to finish his studies in his youth, but he got ahead because he's good with numbers and began to keep books for a warehouse on the docks in San Juan, and later on, as the years went by, he became a partner, always dressed in gray, with a gray half-smile and now with gray hair everywhere. He's so serious he refuses to remember his barefoot adolescent days, running outside the old walls in San Juan and swimming far out in the sea. Don't get tense! And challenging a rival to a swimming race, where far out in the ocean a shark tore off his competitor's leg and he was pulled from the sea screaming "Mami, Mami" . . . And the first thing the man will hang on the wall in his house will be a gray electric clock with black numbers. And the first thing the *Doña* will hang on the wall will be a pink plastic pair of ballet dancers. The first thing the niece will put in her room will be a photograph from the campaign of Governor Hernández Colón, posed to make him look like Jack Kennedy; and she will stare at him for a long time, imagining that she has been selected teacher of the year (because the principal of her school already told her that she had a shot at it); and that she is invited to La Fortaleza, the governor's mansion, with her black hair and red nails cast as nets to catch so handsome a man. The people in K-11 will be received with curiosity.

But all of them will move in at the same time, and since they are all Puerto Ricans they won't be able to stand the sameness of their houses for more than a week and a half. The woman in K-5 will paint the eaves of her roof lilac. The couple in K-7 will paint theirs an elegant green to match the ornamental iron bars they'll order for their carport. The family in K-9 will paint their eaves blue to match their ornamental iron bars, which will be even more ornate than the ones of K-7. And they'll plant two royal palms in the front of their house and a mango tree and a lemon tree in the backyard; they'll place a wrought iron, black French poodle dog, with the letter K and the number 9 on top, on the wall by the front door, and a blue rubber welcome mat, that has "Welcome" printed on it, by the front door. The *Doña* from K-11 plans to paint her eaves yellow, but the niece will be against it because the election will come soon and those sons-of-a-bitch-neighbors from the New Progressive Party painted everything white and blue, so instead she will paint hers shocking red and white to taunt them, and will place many potted poinsettias around her house to bloom Popular Party red at Christmas time.

(The man walks to the lamp and attempts to turn it off. His hand will be stopped with a firm gesture and an even firmer tone of voice ordering, "No, not yet." We retreat a little from their faces and can see the tension in their bodies.)

Afterward we'll have to take them out of their houses and get them together, to get their paths to cross, to intertwine them, because they are too near and yet too far, and without this movement they'd never meet. The occasion will come three weeks later when they don't know each other well yet and they barely murmur when they greet each other, when the lights go out as the result of a terrorist act, as the newspapers will call it the next day, Sunday morning. And the woman from K-5 will run frightened to K-7, but the couple will have gone to the temple for the seven-thirty evening sermon. Then she'll walk to K-9, she, fat and with eyes full of fear, she, who goes everywhere in her gray Volkswagen, but the family left early to see the Ice Show at the coliseum, and the dark street scares her because the lot on the other side of the street, which will be Partenón Avenue when they put up the street sign, is still undeveloped and doesn't yet have identical houses, just woods. And the woman will walk to K-11 at the end of the block, but the *Doña* and her niece have gone out to a séance in which they'll try to communicate with Don Luis Muñoz Rivera to seek guidance about Puerto Rico's future, and only the man is home.

"Who is it?" he'll say when she rings the bell.

"Excuse me for bothering you," she'll say, "I'm your neighbor from the next corner, from K-5, and I came to ask you if you had a candle or a flashlight to lend me. You know, I live alone and . . ." And the man will open the door. His door. The doors will open.

(The camera concentrates on him; then quickly on her, and returns to focus on the man, who smiles sourly and happy at the same time.)

In two more months they'll feel a bit like a community, after exchanging recipes across fences and advice on the best way to plant Zoicia grass so it'll grow better, the neighbors of Block K of the Villa Atenas housing development will call for a meeting with those from Blocks H, I, J, and L to form a group that will go and protest because the Independent Builders Company, the owner and builder of the Villa Atenas housing development, is reneging on the promise in its sales brochure to extend Partenón Avenue so that it connects directly to the expressway, but instead has left the neighbors enclosed in the development, forcing them to drive through four other developments to get to the expressway from Atenas. And that can't be permitted. Someone will suggest a picket line and registering a formal protest with the press because they've already gone four times to the Independent Builders Company and it hasn't paid any attention to them. And their picture will be in the newspaper with all their children, dogs, and all: RESIDENTS OF VILLA ATENAS PROTEST. And from then on they will all be neighbors; all the smells from the kitchens at dusk will mingle together; the sounds of radios, televisions, and record players will be heard together; and their combined voices will echo out to Partenón Avenue, as if they emanated from a single house:

"My tits! I need someone to touch my tits!"

"Damn it, that's all I'll put up with, get out of here right now with that poster."

"Yes, like that, push it in slowly, in and out, in and out."

"We were a big family with many small cousins always living with us; I think I like children for that reason. We were happy in town and when we wanted to, in a flash, we were sliding down the mountainside on yagua leaves and picking fruit from the trees."

"As a kid I slept in a bed with pillars with my brother, but very often he had an urge at night and I could hear him leave the bed and go to the yard. Then, in a little while, I'd hear grandma's pig squealing. Once he thrust it into a plantain leaf and I scared him when I told him 'now the plantains will grow your face on them,' and he got scared because he truly believed me. We went through a lot together, my brother and I."

"I know what it is to hustle washing cars after school and on Saturdays from six to six to have four dollars to take my girlfriend to the movies and to be so exhausted that one day I fell asleep and didn't pick her up. That's how I lost my girlfriend."

"My father made us pray every night. He was strict and if we misbehaved he made us pull down our panties, and he spanked us with his belt and left us kneeling in front of the crucifix in his bedroom."

"Come on Awilda, push little one, push a little, and don't worry about anything, I'll be here until you finish."

"I'd walk through the streets in San Juan and climb uphill to my grandparents' house. They always received me happily and would ask me why I didn't come more often, and they always had rice pudding waiting for me, which was about the only thing they could eat because both of them had no teeth."

"The Lord, the Lord is almighty and he loves and takes care of all of us."

"I hate that town, so dirty and dusty, and all those loafers in the town square screaming things every time a woman goes by."

Finally, the Avenue will be completed, just in time for revelers to drive through for surprise, midnight Christmas parties. By the time Christmas rolls around, on Sunday afternoons, the niece of the man will visit the woman because she'll have an eye on her brother, since it's rumored that he's getting a divorce, and she'll tell the woman about the town she lived in and how much she hated it. The girl from K-7 will get together with the man's *Doña* and the *Doña* will explain the world of the spirits to her, and she'll take the girl to the house of Souls, in Santurce, and on the way the *Doña* will tell her about her big, happy family with many cousins. The Mister's Oldest Son will wash the car of the man's niece because he'll have a crush on her and has heard that she's not hard to get. The Mister's Missus will try to convert the boy from K-7 to Catholicism when she sees him wearing a medallion of the Virgin and she'll have long conversations with him on the porch of her house and she'll tell him about her strict father who spanked her and he'll tell her about the many things he went through with his brother. The Mister will also become friendly with the boy and attempt to get him to vote for the New Progressive Party by trying to convince him that life will be better when Puerto Rico becomes a state, and he will tell the boy how he used to sweat washing cars in his youth. The young woman will teach embroidery to the girl, teaching her very patiently to push the needle in and out, in and out. When Awilda, the hamster, gives birth, the Second Son will give a baby hamster to the young woman and the young woman will baby-sit for the Pampered One when the family goes out, entertaining him with stories about her life in San Juan when she was a girl, and the rice pudding her grandparents fed her.

I tell you it'll be like that. One day the hamster will die and the Mister's *Doña* will want to console the Second Son, telling him that the Lord takes care of all of us even after death. And the Mister will become furious about the poster of Walter Mercado that the little girl will put in her room because that will be it for him; and one afternoon when everyone has gone out and the street is deserted at four o'clock he'll go to pour his heart out to the woman.

She will open the door to her house barefoot because she'll be in the middle of washing the floor, and he'll stare at her bare feet and he'll really see her for the first time, so chubby, a spinster, always willing to drown her sorrows in whiskey, and the family man will come to her. Just like the recently married man came to tell her of his fears. And just as you arrived, though you didn't come to talk. You came today just as you came that night, to dare to remember, to allow you to watch me while I take a bath, to speak to you about sharks that tear off legs, and about my fear of lizards. Come quickly, fondle my white breast, which studied at the Las Madres School, hurry up, your *Doña* is coming back. Here is the recipe she asked me for and tell her I have a *guiro* for our midnight surprise party next weekend.

Turn off the light now because the neighbors are about to come back to their houses, and be careful you don't stain your clothes with whiskey like that other time; come on, finish up, because when you finish we'll have to write

THE END

to start again to shoot the film, for the lights and the shadows to come alive; the shadows of silence and your silence and mine will cover everything and the scene with my round face will begin when I speak and I say that everything will start on a greenish day in which, at the same time, four identical cars will approach the Phase Number One of Villa Atenas housing development, which will have been built by now, with identical white houses on each block, one beside the other, one beside the other.

Translated by Carmen C. Esteves

Teresa Irene

ANGELA
HERNÁNDEZ

She had just turned three when she disappeared for the first time. It happened on the very same day her father died. She was so little—the youngest of nine children—that no one noticed her absence, busy as they were in casting off their grief.

They were stewing a calf in huge cauldrons. The relatives attending the funeral awaited their share of the tender victuals in the spirit of a feast rather than a wake. The promise of free food nurtured a dark sympathy with death. Confronted with the news, however, their better natures instantly blossomed; forgetting their stomachs, they all spilled out in an expansive search.

The alarm had been raised at dinnertime by a distant relative as they were getting ready to serve the mourners, starting with the children. She had questioned them first. They knew nothing. She made the rounds of the house, asking left and right. No one had seen her for hours.

They looked under the beds. They searched the barn, the cupboards, the yard, the eaves, exploring every likely or unlikely corner. They lit rosewood torches, hurling them down the latrine. The nauseating bottom exposed the immutable ebb and flow of a nest of worms.

In any case, the hole was too deep, a man observed—he had helped the father dig it out—and with the years it had been in use, traces of any bulky shape piercing that undulating tide of filth would be immediately obliterated. Chea, the girl's godmother, cried out, horrified, falling onto the floor as if stabbed by a dagger of wind.

For the moment the deceased was disregarded. The girl's mother, having suffered consecutive attacks of pain ablaze with fury, seemed to recover with the news of her daughter's disappearance. Her torture had hit bottom, unveiling an unyielding clearheadedness. She divided the people in small groups to search the surrounding area. Meanwhile, accompanied by Blanca, the eldest daughter, and by her brother Berto, she followed the path to the river. A dark hope guided her intuition toward the deepest and farthest corners, toward the deep pool where the children were prohibited from bathing.

It was deceptively crystallike. It sparkled like a gigantic diamond pierced by the sunlight filtered through the tall branches of its venerable cupola. From the shore one could see the bottom in great detail. It was easy to trace the path of a timorous crayfish along the white stones of the crystal-clear riverbed.

The best swimmers approached the pool of the Jaquey Crossing, as it is known, with caution. Its bed was traversed by underwater currents forming treacherous whirlpools whose circular rages were unfathomable from the surface.

She was at the bottom. Her very short hair mingled with the naturalness of the algae. Lying slantwise on a current, her white satin skirt flowed invariably to the right. Otherwise, a perfect stillness formed the elements of the tableau. Blanca screamed, suffocating the tremors threatening to overcome her: She's dead. Berto anticipated his mother's reaction, grabbing her with all his might. She looked peaceful, watching the childish tattoo on the bed of the pool, as if it were the consummation of an inexorable dream.

In a matter of seconds the diamond of water was surrounded by people and sobs. The most varied opinions displaced the initial surprise: She may be alive for all we know. Why is she not floating? Find Genaro, he knows all about drownings. Take the mother away from here. Bring some rope. Don't let anyone jump in without tying them securely. Pull that boy away from here.

I don't need any rope, Genaro said as he dove in with the ancient grace of a proven winner. He never returned.

Two old men arrived with the rope, the only two to have remained in the house with the body. They took over the task of rescue with the patience that comes from self-assurance. The deceased remained behind, enjoying the tranquil silence. Death was long; life possessed the urgency of the ephemeral.

They pulled the girl out, but Genaro disappeared among the caves carved by the deep currents.

Her eyes were open. She looked without surprise at the tens of relatives and neighbors watching her with solemn amazement. She breathed naturally. I want milk, she said, and she yawned as if she had slept too much. At that very instant they discovered the eyes of Teresa Irene, or, better yet, they understood what they saw. They are pink, they are green, bluer than the sky, they are the color of the afternoon as it vanishes. Unsure of their own perceptions, they had nonetheless no choice but to admit the evidence before them; Teresa Irene gathered all colors in her eyes. Grains of water and light; the rainbow in them. Except that unlike the rainbow, the colors in her eyes alternated, configuring a disk in whose radial stripes it was impossible to determine the space occupied by the violets, blues, oranges, or any other components of the naked light.

Teresa Irene, naturalness itself in her acts, was interpreted, thought about, X-rayed from supernatural or abnormal points of reference. Her mother hung a jet-stone charm from her neck and an amulet with a clove of garlic on the wrist of her left hand. One of her brothers followed her every time she strayed farther than two hundred meters from the house. At the same time they kept all the other children away from her, so she learned to entertain herself with the chickens and the other birds in the yard, following meticulously the swimming lessons of the ducklings in the pond. She spoke little, but observed everything with an acute innocence disconcerting to the adults.

More than once they stopped her on the narrow path that led to the river. They excused her from fetching water and she was never allowed to accompany her sisters when they went to the bath. With time they stopped marveling at her rapture when they found her leaning against the water basin or with her ears glued to the earthen jar, as if she were listening attentively to a message. She seemed to enjoy sun showers in her own particular way and laughed, fascinated, at the tales of weddings between witches and princes with which Ana Inocencia adorned those moments.

When she was seven she disappeared again. Without hesitation, the mother and two of her sons set out for the Jaquey Crossing pool. The mother walked ahead, teary-eyed and strong, carrying the weakness of her eyes in the vigor of her long legs, hardened by the farmwork and the everyday bustle. She recalled the episode of four years before, she remembered old Genaro, and an icy furor stirred up her nerves.

Alarmed and sweat-soaked, they traversed the bank of the river, scrutinizing in vain the bed of the pool. The translucent diamond displayed its usual inhabitants.

With her skirt tucked under her knees the mother skipped along, her gaze buried in the water. From day to day she had been steeling herself against something uncertain concerning Teresa Irene. The obsessions, the questions fixed on the girl, who nonetheless kept growing oblivious to agitations and lucubrations, had inspired in the mother an overflowing love. She loved her more and more; she loved her with a love mixed with pain that was beyond her understanding, a love exacerbated by the enigma, by the misfortune of seeing her hovering over the threshold of a world where she yielded no influence. She adored her with the unconfessed notion that her late husband blossomed in some way in the rainbow of her gaze.

Her spirit prey to an unendurable despair, she prayed to God not to take her away, not now, because it would be unbearable not to see her again, never to see herself reflected again in the purity of her chronic circles, not to hold tightly against her the small body that returned each caress with warm fervor. No, not now, my God, please; holiest of virgins, protect her, and I vow to have her wear a habit, I will drape her in purple as a constant reminder that she belongs only to you.

They found her in the stream, on a stretch closer to the house than the mouth of the river, lying at a precarious intersection of the water flow. She was asleep under the shelter of the bouquets of braided shadow.

In the eyes of Ana Inocencia, a year older than Teresa Irene, her sister was an exquisite being. Together they invented games and figures, sharing a language made of graphics drawn on the ground; queries about the intricacies of the birdnests; drawings made of pebbles and an entire arsenal of begonias, baby eggplants, pear and almond seeds, and fragments of china and stripes of fabric discarded by their mother.

Yet, even in their complicity, they were different. A difference notable to the adults but insignificant to those whose ages predisposed them to amazement.

Seated on the ground, they took pleasure in modeling clay figurines. They experimented for a long time before they achieved stable mixtures. Sometimes excessive water led to a weak mud with which they painted pieces of rock and branches. At other times, believing to have achieved the perfect combination, they molded figurines which, when exposed to the sun. turned porous and brittle. Ana Inocencia did not disguise her disappointment, turning over molds and crumbling the primitive effigies with her feet. With absolute serenity, Teresa Irene reorganized the ingredients, arranging them to start again, as if the amusement rested precisely in the experimentation and not in the final result.

Small pots, round-headed dolls with cigarlike arms, were proud works for Ana Inocencia. Teresa Irene, on the other hand, molded inexplicable figures which, even today, more than twenty-five years later, are kept in a handful of houses of the old and now-changed community. Inverted prisms sustained by solid planes, from whose surfaces rose multitudes of bushes of equal size and identical leaves;

houses burdened by the weight of oranges, papayas, sapodillas, and other fruits; guinea hens blindfolded with pieces of mirrors, and necklaces of butterflies, lamps placed on the headboard of a sleeping child; balls with multiple parameters shifting toward a post on whose top there is a two-petal flower; colts, peacocks, and dogs warming themselves in front of a fire; and many other figures with unexplainable and harmonious contours, sprinkled here and there with spots of turquoise-colored earth.

In a commonplace child, the conglomerate of heterogenous figurines would have been seen as the product of a prolific childish fantasy. In Teresa Irene it was a confirmation of her exceptionality. With time she would begin to understand that people who are different from most are forced to act in a more ordinary manner than others. But when she came to understand this, she didn't care anymore.

The first and most painful warning of her isolation came with her sister's gradual withdrawal. Once childhood was behind them, the wordless complicity in play and exploration was no longer possible. Ana Inocencia wanted to share the secret of the hardening buttons flowering on her chest, the dark wool appearing under her arms, the itching of a maturing sexuality. She approached Teresa Irene with a certain mischievousness, inquiring about the mystery unfolding in their bodies and its relation to their mother's prohibition against eating fruit: "I am about to develop soon. You still have a long way to go. It is as if I were being set aflame from many sides. You still have neither hair nor tits." Teresa Irene replied with a sweet gesture of the mouth. She did not formulate any comment, however. Their circumstances were inevitably diverging.

In her early teenage years Teresa Irene conceived the notion of becoming a saint.

Except for a certain degree of muscular subtlety, her development was normal, but relatives and neighbors were bent on attributing oddities to her. The word spread that water flowed from her breasts. Her first period came when she was fourteen. Instead of blood, she menstruated warm water. As her cousin Emilio attested, when her mother tried to extract a chigger from a swollen toe, her face was splattered by a fine sand, little fish laid in the pregnant toe. Instead of hair under her arms and on her pubis, she had threads of algae. Teresa Irene didn't even suspect what was said about her.

The truth was that, at a glance, the only unusual thing about her was the color of her eyes. Having grown up in solitude—Ana Inocencia had been her only friend—it never occurred to her to boast of this distinction, as she never expressed annoyance at wearing light purple all the time, while her sisters displayed an ample spectrum of colors in their clothing.

The visitors that came to her house to see her had multiplied with the installation in the neighborhood of a subsidiary of the national oil industry, to whom the peasants came to sell their peanuts. Many came by the house with the pretext of asking for a glass of water or to use the outhouse. This perturbed her.

That was when she decided to become a saint. Not with the purpose of featuring in altars, or having devotees or aiding the destitute, or of being closer to God, but a saint so that she would not rot and could stay in the water and remain intact, to return to the water crystals and see the world eternally filtered through them, perfumed by their freshness.

Through its beneficial crystals the greens homogenized themselves into oblique sensations, the stones softened peacefully, the chamomiles diluted in immaculate stains. They assimilated the rumors of suffering, the urgency of hunger and loneliness, imprinting a timeless rhythm to everything that lodged behind its hospitable curtain.

As the visitors snooped into her eyes, she studied the Virgin of

Miracles, the Virgin of Altagracia, the Virgin of All Saints, of Lourdes, of Carmen, of Fatima.

Weary of the daily siege and devoid of a clear formula for sainthood, she began to disappear at dawn, returning at dusk. On these occasions her eyes dimmed into black and no one pursued her to look into them.

She discovered a singular place where she spent her days, submerged in the deepest spot, hidden by branches bending over the very surface of the water. An enormous pine tree grew tall nearby; a bit farther off a saman spilled over. Lilies floated on the banks. In routine navigation, leaves and light flowers flowed by in slow advance. Besides the unfolding greens there was the expansion of corollas, the barks metamorphosing into unimaginable graphic combinations; besides the hint of a breeze hidden in the wings of a mockingbird, and of the winged humility of the *rolitas,* she would have liked to see people, to enjoy their company, hear their laughter mingle with the flow of the water. To see brilliant and fervent glances, like those of the huge water crystals when they sacrifice themselves to the sun. To see in human hands the planetary geometry of the barks.

She knew it to be impossible. People cannot look without asking, they cannot observe without seeking ciphered messages that predict the course of their existence; they cannot live according to the whims of nature.

She ceased wearing shoes and ingesting food just when she turned sixteen. She roamed in the open sun through the thorniest areas. Those who managed to see her, extremely thin, on her wanderings amid brambles and bush, with her long, tangled hair covering her back, with her eyes like a display of the finest gems, with her elegant forehead and her tattered purple clothes, with her leathery skin and her hands groping the air as if she were blind, with her mouth like a conjunction of antique smiles, said that she looked less like a saint than an extravagance of the forest, another offspring of the pine trees and the ironweeds, a new species of comfrey, a prolongation of the cascade, the materialization of some delirium.

She grew so thin she almost disappeared; she was seen outlined against the trees like a spark in a ruined dawn. On the thirty-first day of December, as the arrival of a new year was celebrated, she took the path to the Jaquey Crossing pool. She was so weak that she crawled part of the way. They didn't look for her until the following day.

As thirteen years before, the mother organized a search party. In the same way as before, she took the path to the river accompanied by Blanca and Berto. The waters of the big diamond looked the same as ever: still, blindly crystalline. A few lilacs floated on the opposite bank. On the waterbed there was the purple tattoo of a sleeping lady. The long mane detoured to the right, as if carried away by an invisible current.

The neighborhood people arrived; they wanted to bring rope to bring her up. This time the mother demurred. Instead, she lit candles, recited the Creed, and improvised an altar with white sheets over the bushes.

By the next day Teresa Irene had disappeared from her aquatic bed.

Since then the place has been called Ciguapa Pool. The mother dislikes the name, it seems pagan and inconsiderate to her. But she is calm and accepting. She thinks her daughter is intact somewhere. Besides, she became convinced a long time before that Teresa Irene could appreciate the world only through water crystals.

No person would ever again bathe in the Ciguapa Pool. The diaphanous lagoon was consecrated exclusively to the rainbow. The people know that the light is thirsty. When the tense indoor dryness becomes stifling, she sheds her clothes, confidently displaying her dawns, and ventures to take a drink of water.

Subsequent generations were privileged to hold one secret fewer and one more landscape. Under the drizzle, hand in hand with their grandparents, children watch the trajectory of the thirsty light, until they catch her diving in to take a long drink.

Once her pretensions broke all grounds. She went to drink water and resolved to remain dressed in the eyes of a girl called Teresa Irene.

Translated by Lizabeth Paravisini-Gebert

Aunt Luisita

BARBARA
JACOBS

Why is it that I have always been suspicious, distrustful, and, therefore, as a defense mechanism, somewhat cynical? A very determined high school teacher, as a young and according to my observations still naive psychology scholar, assures me that because of this, because I am the way I am, certain things happen to me. In other words, since I keep imagining that the other people are cheaters, to put it mildly, when I come to meet them I do nothing but end up being cheated by them. To such a conclusion I can hold up the following question: if I imagined that others were honorable, when I got to meet them, would I end up winning? But I never get a satisfactory answer, since the truth of the matter is that whether I consider them swindlers or not, they will cheat me; or, whether I think them trustworthy or not, it is I who catches them cheating others. And so it is not strange that I am short-changed when I pay a cabdriver or cashier at a restaurant—I understand it. But what about my cynicism? Well, I don't know why, but to date it has been limited to jeering at my aggressor without mercy, but only once I am far enough away from his reach. Then I jeer at the fact he smells like *pulque* mixed with beans, or at her hem that's come undone; I mock him or her, I said, but not in his or her presence; it would be undignified of me to do so, I theorize.

Since things are the way they are, my family thinks I am somewhat unbearable. I am always alert, on the defensive, predicting small catastrophes. In short, I am a kind of party pooper, whether or not there is a party.

The other day, to give you a better idea, was my mother's birthday. She loves to invite over all the aunts (of which there are about twenty), though every year she says it will be the last time she celebrates her birthday, claiming she would rather let the occasion pass unobserved. Nevertheless, I hope she doesn't mean it, because it is precisely on her birthday that she is the happiest and most energetic I ever see her, and I like seeing her that way, though I cannot help myself from putting a grain of salt to sadden her, even just a little, I can't help it.

She prepares everything with candid enthusiasm, but with the experience that her "savoir-vivre" specially gives her, as it is reasonably said. If she lays out a pink silk tablecloth (interwoven with silver threads), she dresses, as if only by coincidence, in pink; she sets out a pink dinner service, naturally, and some matching candles. Finally, she makes sure to tell my eldest sister to suggest to our dad to send her pink roses, and Dad, who adores her (my eldest sister), will obey. And in the wink of an eye, so long as said wink is deliberate and slow, the house is perfumed and lit and faces turn smiling and the door is opened wide, everything awaiting the sweet herd, or well-groomed army, or gracious group of aunts, or, as I dryly refer to them, the *auntesque*. My mother, pinkish in more than one sense and place, gives a final angelic touch to her paradisiacal table.

"It is going to rain," I tell her suddenly, as I, despite all my principles and abilities, help her place the napkins (guess what color) to the left of the plates.

The truth of the matter is that my mother now hardly ever responds immediately; she prefers to keep accumulating motives, like a balloon, so that some night when I have a cold or am for whatever reason defenseless and at her mercy, she will suddenly explode with flying colors, letting out in one burst an entire discourse that—were it not for my memory—by now I would know from beginning to end, but which more or less starts by exposing, one by one, my cutting remarks, those torn rags laid out in the sun, and ends with the following dark moral, a common denominator to all my faults: if you envision life to be black, she tells me, it will be black, and on those occasions I am assailed by the suspicion my mother might be in league with my high school teacher in order to threaten and destabilize my future.

In any case, it did rain that afternoon, though it was neither the rainy season nor, much less, anyone's wish. Here in Mexico City (written with capital letters so I won't be hit across the knuckles with a ruler by the teachers who stick to my memory, as if they were flies, no matter how hard I try to shake them off) that is how it is. It rains when the rain wants to vent, forget London or the Tropics, which I don't even know for sure what or where they are. That afternoon it rained and my mother's tea was on the verge of being a failure.

Well, not if you see things the way I do, since I believe the rain had wanted to pour (regardless of its own sorrows) just to honor my hunch, which satisfied me to the point of wearing a grin from ear to ear and my ears are rather far apart because I have a wide face. It had me so satisfied and happy, as I was saying, that one of the aunts, avidly, with her eyes opened wide, like those of an old maid determined not to miss out on anything that two people could be shamelessly doing under a tree, and, I imagine, almost savoring the words of her question and my awaited response, did not dally in inquisitionally asking, acting as if she would guard the secret but taking pains to pay attention to every detail in order to be able to fully divulge it; she asked me, as I was saying, if I was not completely and fully in love, I suppose because lovers do not stop smiling, seeing everything, as they do, through rose-colored glasses, and I could already see her gossiping to the rest of the aunts about my response, or any other that perhaps would have brought her more delight.

The torrent of rain was so unexpected that not one of the aunts came prepared, but, since they had been punctual, they had the good fortune not to get wet; to enjoy it, almost, from the soft cushions of the armchairs that their abundant and adorned bodies sat back in at around five-thirty. Any day now they would risk the rain impeding their arrival; any day now they would miss one of the receptions to which my mother would invite them.

I say my mother should be the guest of honor, and not, as it always is, that the guests of honor should turn out to be the aunts: my mother attends to them, making sure everything is to their liking, only to have them not respond in kind. My mother says that the pleasure lies in giving, but no one quite believes her, or is it that the *auntesque* does not feel pleasure at receiving and receiving and receiving? Of course, probably, if I were like my mother, I suppose I would love them as she does, but in view of the fact that I am only like myself, I only love them in my own way, which is with suspicion and mistrust.

I was saying, all the aunts arrived dry and on time, with the exception of Aunt Luisita (that is her name; it is not a nickname), a corpulent woman of some fifty-odd years of age. Aunt Luisita lives God-knows-where; she has never invited anyone to her house and, although they all conjecture about where and how she must live, they know for sure only the way there and the intersections, which are, at most, where she will let one drop her off when she has been offered a ride. Sometimes she says she took three buses to get to our house; sometimes only one; on other occasions it has been four. I think she lives around the corner and creates a drama about the thousand buses and the endless obstacles and the number of intersections (they change according to where the newspaper vendor decides to install himself: if it is on this corner, she asks to be left on that other one) in order to confuse, to arouse our pity. This is why I don't like her as much as I could.

She doesn't do but what all men say women do; surely, they have heard my aunt, and as they all lack the patience analytical exercises require, they all generalize. In other words, Aunt Luisita, besides inspiring pity, is like a man in that she never stops talking about herself: what I said, what I did, what I thought, what I felt. It is as if she were psychoanalyzing herself in public, and in addition, for free, every time she would have an audience that voluntarily, accidentally, or inescapably, would listen.

It would be less tedious if she would, for a change, break from

her monotonous habit and on occasion, so as to maintain our association with the science of the psyche, refer instead to dreams, even if
she would invent it on the spot. Let us imagine her dreaming of her
boss raping her; she is actually shrieking but her yelps are coquettish,
and she is lifting her skirt, according to her, with modesty and discretion, and the surprisingly but decidedly repentant boss leaving her
ruffled and undressed. Certainly, one must suppose that in the telling
of the dream she would invert the roles: the boss would be the all-
excited one, and so as not to scare us, she would keep the role of the
penitent.

The point is, she arrived late and soaking wet, as for the wrinkles, she's had them for as long as I can remember. Furthermore, she
was furious: so much so that her appearance, in my view, deformed
because of her enormity, did not even seem ridiculous to anyone. A
real silence ensued; not the kind that covers a stifled laugh, and by
the way, my family is lighthearted, laughing at any stupidity, although some of us cross too far over the line, set by the confraternity
with our relatives, and as a result become known as first-class, tasteless, bad-humored folks.

In her fury she lashed out by saying that to begin with, she
had had to take ten buses, and furthermore at her age and with all
her problems (according to me, in proportion to her Valkyrian
size), and what was more, with the rainstorm having fallen on her,
she was not in the mood neither to think it fair nor to forget it
happened. She became so pathetic that, I am certain, she stirred
compassion in some of the other aunts who, considering everyone
had his or her burden, did not after all have to work at a nuts and
bolts (for export) factory, or periodically fall ill (of illnesses that, I
don't know why, I feel are fake), or look as aged as she: I imagine
they thought of all these things when they saw her. For a moment,
even the candles, in the center of the long, rectangular table,
seemed to be on the verge of melting and their wicks of extin-

guishing, and the candlesticks almost tarnishing as a result of their pure, sheer sadness.

Nevertheless, with the ability of the healthy not to suffer more than is required, the *auntesque* ridded itself of all the nuisances (of rain, age, and general bad luck), piling it all on Aunt Luisita, and free at last, resumed its carefree, indifferent, and pompous chatter.

Only my mother, prudent and impartial Good Samaritan that she is, and above all the perfect housewife determined to save her tea at any cost, because, what if she seriously decided not to celebrate another birthday, then it would be important, for the sake of memories, to really splurge on *this* party; to go *all* out; to avoid, at all costs, anyone ruining *this* occasion: not I, or Aunt Luisita, or anything (I know this list of possibilities passed through her adorable mind like a flock of handsome sea gulls flying through a white foamy cloud); only she, I was saying, was capable of coming to Aunt Luisita's rescue.

In desperate situations my mother knows how to be practical, and what she did in that desperate case was to take screwy Aunt Luisita—who, through her sparse, small, wet eyelashes, saw that her audience had gradually begun to lose sympathy for her—by the hand, as if Aunt Luisita had suddenly turned into a big girl who had wet her pants in front of supposedly polite company, which was actually more critical than an old bachelor, and took my aunt to the bathroom, where she helped dry her and gave her a good alcohol rub.

The party, consequently, continued, and judging by the annoying bursts of laughter I heard from where I was in the kitchen, where I watched the rain lessen and where, to undepress myself, since so much fuss and rejoicing, when not mine, sooner or later throw me into an abyss of profound dejection and bitterness, I was concentrated on eating more and more salted crackers, pastries, and finger sandwiches; I gather it was a great success. My mother's parties always are. And my prediction of rain, with its subsequent crystallization and everything, hardly disturbed that happiness.

At some point, drop by drop, the rain ceased and the aunts began to leave. Their chauffeurs, not necessarily their employers' lovers, though in this last respect I have my doubts concerning more than one of my reliable aunts; the chauffeurs, I was saying, began to arrive to pick them up with the umbrellas that they, like the well-trained employees that they are, had gone to fetch, and since, because of the weather, they had not been able to amuse themselves by polishing their already polished vehicles, which were practically moving homes to them.

One of the aunts offered to take Aunt Luisita to her house, perhaps, in part, because of the unworn curiosity that gnawed at the obstinate mind of the entire *auntesque:* where did Aunt Luisita live? But Aunt Luisita, who had a nose for everything, skillfully skirted the issue: she graciously accepted the offer, since at her age, with her problems, traveling alone at night was the equivalent to opening the door to an assailant; she accepted, but much to the frustration of the aunt who volunteered to drive her, priding herself ahead of time in being the first to see the unknown house, Aunt Luisita informed her that she was headed somewhere else, in any case, not to her uncertain domicile.

My mother, I don't know if only so that it wouldn't be held against her if she didn't, or out of yet another fit of courtesy, or simply because she truly is a love, lent her, though the rain had stopped, a raincoat she had bought during a recent trip, one she wore only on exceptional occasions, when my father looked her up and down, thumbs under his armpits, and told her with pride and passion: "Beautiful!" only in another language, since he is a foreigner.

I did not resist the temptation, and when Aunt Luisita was far away enough, I told my mother, "How much do you want to bet she won't return it?" since Aunt Luisita had tried to refuse it, saying, "Don't bother," with that special and unique way of hers of simultaneously knitting her brow and puckering her nose, like a rabbit, which made me realize that sooner or later she would cheat my mother.

"I'll return it tomorrow," she had clucked from the doorway, strutting and swaggering, wrapped in the fine, new raincoat.

"I'll bet whatever you want, Mom, that you'll never see it again," I insisted.

Then, as if I had been at her complete mercy because of the flu, or something like it, my mother, her eyes bright and shiny, took the opportunity to tell me that I had a lot to learn about other people, and that I was undeserving of anyone's affection; with that, she thought she would put me in my place or cause me to react.

When she is forceful with me, I think she believes she is humiliating me: that, having had to scold me, she hurts me. I suppose she does it this way, which in case she wants to know, is so unbecoming to her, because she must have heard this is how one arrives at maturity, by receiving plenty of blows (even if they are moral ones), each one a little harder, or God only knows what she must have heard, but the fact is that lately my mother's eyes light up when she scolds me, while, on the other hand, when she scolded me when I was a child, her eyes were filled with tears (how unfortunate that people should change for the worse).

One day she told me that when I had a daughter I would pay for every little thing I had done to her; and then I inquired if she were paying with me for everything she had done to her own mother, one bad deed to another, but she did not respond. It was like the time one of my mother's former teachers, a nun (when will mothers overcome their zeal for passing on, on top of everything else, their schools and their teachers?), would use my mother to illustrate the qualities of the ideal student: obedient, courteous, affectionate, diligent, and, directing her comments to me, she dolefully complained, "What did your mother do to deserve you?" and I answered, "She married my father," and she did not respond either, so I thought, "Ah, so Mother learned from her to not answer my questions." And then I was convinced of the adage "Like father, like son," as it refers, of course, to those two, since as far as I'm concerned, that law, and all laws for that matter, meet with my tenacious resistance.

But that afternoon, when my mom told me about my having a lot to learn about people and about my not deserving anyone's affection, the truth is I had an ugly feeling at the pit of my stomach. I felt as if a blackish cat were tearing my veins apart and sliding its claws over them, because it felt like something had ripped at my insides, though I'm not so sure it involved precisely my veins: I have never had an outstanding grasp of anatomy, history, or math, but in matters of love and affection and in knowing character I had rather always believed, from the very depths of my being, that I was lucid. But my mother made me think twice about it. It could be, after all, that it was in those areas precisely where I was really confounded.

I mentioned I did feel awful. And more so because I remembered, and in this case my memory did not fail me, that it was Aunt Luisita and no other who always wished me well not only on my birthdays but also on my saint day (even when the Church demoted, among others, the great lady, patron of artillerymen and firefighters, who bears my name); also—and why is it I had never had this opportune recollection before?—it was she who called when I was sick, and here I must open a huge parenthesis (I have almost always been sick: it is either the appendix, or the tonsils, or a slightly deviated septum, or an intestinal infection, or countless other illnesses: countless as far as actual number and as far as the inability to recount them. This last one exists for two reasons: fear that if I relate them they will become real, and sheer laziness at facing when I reveal them, real or unreal, the fact that no one will believe me. But among many, one worthy of mentioning is the pain in the extreme superior portion of the left part of the chest, for instance, or the blotches that appear on my skin, or) which now I have closed; Aunt Luisita, then, called when I was ill and told my mother, "Tell so-and-so (it embarrasses me to say my name) I am praying for her."

This recollection was as fitting as a ring to a finger; only, the ring was not my size. Nevertheless, thanks to the aforementioned memory, my feelings sort of went crazy: suddenly, they were affably guilty, that is, sociable with guilt, sweet with guilt, kind with guilt, cordial with guilt toward Aunt Luisita, who prayed for me; and toward humanity, who did nothing for me, not that I was aware of, but try to cheat me. I felt a halo of goodness was in one way crushing my suspicion, my mistrust, and, in another way, I felt my body, my life, because of all the guilt they carried, turn me into a kind of mined field, and I wish my tongue had slipped and said momed field, for Mom, overindulgent as it might seem, with a capital O and all.

The point is I felt I had learned the lesson; from now on, I thought, I will do nothing but carry myself along the lines of the nun's ideal; that is to say, exactly like my mother, anything to be worthy of someone's affection, whosoever it would be, or at the very least, worthy of the chaste, devote, fervent, noble prayers of Aunt Luisita, dear Auntie Luisita.

That night I made my first list of resolutions, among which the most important one was the already mentioned transformation of my ways with others (also included were the following: to get up earlier to organize my day, to work hard to be in a good mood, and finally, to refrain from jeering at my teachers so I could pass my examinations: I made it a point to stop calling the psychology teacher by the nickname Wet Chicken Head). And when I woke up, it could be said that I began a new life.

A few days later, as I was coming out of a movie theater with a friend (was I deserving of his affection?), or maybe it was that we were about to go in and we decided it was better not to (was I earning his affection?), or I don't recall if what happened was that we simply could not get tickets (had I been deemed worthy of his affection?), but in any case, I thought I had seen Aunt Luisita in the distance.

My first impulse was to pretend I hadn't seen her, since people do not change easily and my suspicions and mistrust were the first allies that came to my defense. Furthermore, and I don't know why, but having a family is sometimes inhibiting, and more so if it consists of aunts (and more so, logically, if they number more than twenty), and I did not want my friend to see I had aunts and much less *that* one.

But then my list of resolutions called out. I was also encouraged by the thought of my mother's pleasure (after the surprise) when she found out; Aunt Luisita, touched by it, would breathlessly tell her about my good behavior. If I would dare to set into action my good intentions, if I dared to go greet my aunt, whom I imagined all confused, my definite redemption would be forthcoming.

So, like an automaton, getting through the crowd (it was not such a crowd, but the idea of getting through appeals to me and one can only truly enjoy doing so if there is a crowd), I was coming closer, determined to greet her even if I blushed and my voice were inaudible and I did not know which one should be introduced to whom, my friend to my aunt or my aunt to my friend.

Nevertheless, something stronger than all the aforementioned, something stronger than my resolutions, than my spirit, and even than the concrete difficulties I had butted up against, detained me.

The minute I saw her clearly, that is, really saw her, I was stuck. I stayed, then, at a distance, looking at her as if I were hypnotized. I half heard my friend tell me to wait for him, as he was going to get the car, or whatever, and I just stayed put.

It was her. It was not that when I saw her in detail I would have believed I had only thought to have seen her, that it had been a mirage that, because of my resolutions, would have been convenient, to once and for all have the chance to put the good intentions into apt and gracious practice. It was her, definitely; none other than my good aunt Luisita.

She was arm in arm with another woman (Aunt Luisita was not a spinster, or a widow, or a divorcee, or even married; she, and of all the ladies I know only she, was surrounded by an even greater mystery, which had not been revealed to my sister and I until we got the period: in my family, we were informed of the usual gossip about our distant and closest ancestors only little by little, the process like that of a slow hourglass. This was how we learned Aunt Luisita's marriage had been annulled, though the reason for it to have been, I am sure, we will not know until they deem adequate to accept we are no longer virgins; that is, not only after we have married, but when it's evident a child has been born from our wombs; since, not until the actual moment of childbearing, the thought of a possible annulment for possibly not having consummated the marriage would be hanging over us. Don't they know there are those who give birth even as virgins? Have they forgotten the antonomastic Virgin of Virgins?).

Now, Aunt Luisita and the other woman were chatting and chatting, Aunt Luisita with her shrill voice (uncommon in corpulent women, but present in related amounts in her), which I suppose she also had in her youth, since, even though Mother continually assures us Aunt Luisita was quite beautiful then, the case of her grating voice, I am sure, was brought on when she was nothing more than a random combination of genes, just like those that created her bowleggedness.

The other woman, I believe, was one of Aunt Luisita's coworkers, since she had the bored expression that comes from listening to another all day long, every day, if that other person is dull and talks too much, of course, and if, even worse, she always relates the same sorts of things, and if, much worse even, those things are boring in and of themselves, common places that only common people keep frequenting and frequenting.

They were so absorbed in their conversation (that is, Aunt Luisita was so absorbed in her own, since the other woman was absorbed only in her boredom, I believe, self-pitying herself, with that canine passivity of those who believe to do so is their lot in life) that like those who cannot kill two birds with one stone, at some point they could not keep walking, wherever it was they were going, and there was no choice for them but to keep their backs to the window of a bookstore, one of those ever-present bookstores next to all and ever one of the city's movie theaters, always dusty and deserted, and always on the verge of closing.

Conversation was for Aunt Luisita, I may assure you, just like a scalpel is for a surgeon (compulsively active, even if incompetent), like a saw to a carpenter (compulsively active, even if inexperienced), like a bullet to a hunter (compulsively active, even if cruel), and, as a result, whoever listened to her became the patient, the wood, the hare, that is to say, the plain victim.

So that's where we were: I, paralyzed, watching Aunt Luisita torment the other woman, and now, since my good intentions had finally been scattered by what I will soon tell you, I was satisfied to watch and listen while I waited for my friend, who by the way is such a music lover, and particularly such a Mozart fan, that he has baptized his car with the name Tamino.

To stop beating around the bush, I will once and for all tell you what detained me. It was, in short, what she was wearing and what she told her friend or companion, or at this point whatever you want to call her, about what she was wearing; it was long but I heard it clearly and in its entirety; at this point my ear was like a magnet, and her voice the only metal around.

"Listen," she squeaked in the woman's ear, "I have been making sacrifices for my family, when they do have money, and look, they barely got enough together to give me this"—and she tugged at what she was wearing with a scornful gesture—"listen—it is not warm or water repellent, this useless rag, and look, look"—she forced the woman to look and look—"it does not even fit me. What do you think about this?"

And I don't know what else she must have told her afterward, since my beating temples entered into a competition with the palpitations of my heart; I boiled with rage, I sweated so much (hands, head, chest) that I asked God for my friend to be delayed while moving Tamino from its parking space; I did not want him to notice how I sweat and have it be the reason for his dumping me. "She sweats too much," he would tell his friends in explanation as to why he had so masterfully left a young woman who was so—do I seem likable to you? So I heard what Aunt Luisita said about the raincoat my mother had lent her days before. I heard the whole of it. Though it is said those revelations, so powerful· and complete, the damaged person never experiences fully, I have already warned I am an exception to the rule.

But the worst part, and it seemed that no worse thing could have spilled the glass of bile, was that our gazes, my aunt's and mine, met. The instant we saw one another eye to eye (mine are green), and it was not a wink, only lasted a very brief fraction of a second, but it was long enough for us to see each other.

It was as if I were turning on a Ferris wheel, everything around me was spinning, and as if from the heavens—it seemed so incredible to me—I had seen someone who, having seen me, had felt as if she were part of hell—knew herself burned. It could be said that each one of us had the other at her mercy; what she saw, my situation, that is, was the innocent one; because what I had seen was as impure as a rubbish dump. I felt the impulse to scream, "Luisita!" and not because this name were more just and fitting to her stature, but for other reasons, ones with more weight and proportion.

My friend, who had the perceptions that all gentlemen are capable of, did not notice anything; he simply opened the door of the 1975 blue Volkswagen bug, and I got in, focusing on, I suppose to distract myself, the cuffs of his shirt, which bore a pair of new cuff links engraved with the initials A.M., which are his initials (within parenthesis: he likes to say that in the evenings he exchanges them for a pair with the initials P.M.). Suddenly, I came back to reality and said, "They are going to run her over."

Used to hearing me make foolish remarks, my friend only laughed to himself, like someone who intuits another has made a joke but in reality has not understood what the other has said and it is almost, almost, as if he did not care either way. And then he exclaimed, "Poor old hags!" when he saw how another Volkswagen (he couldn't remember exactly if the license plates read 516 or 915) passed, as if on purpose, over a puddle, the kind that always seem to be on corners (especially if it has rained, or if the city's drainage isn't working, or if the pavement is not level and creates potholes where the water—rainwater, drainage water, water from the buckets of clean people who throw on to the street the water with which they have cleaned their shops, their cafeteria, or their houses, places that were dirty and are now clean—had found a kind of cozy refuge), and as a result of the work of the tire along with the speed at the moment of contact and the muddy water (is that how the law of physics goes, one of them, anyone of them?), combined with the sheer pleasure (an essential human element), it splattered and dirtied and angered two women who were going to cross the street in a hurry, one of them wearing a raincoat and the other with a bored look on her face, which for a fraction of a millisecond turned frightened, or indignant, just like mine.

Translated by Marisella Veiga

BARBARA JACOBS

A Family Man

VLADY
KOCIANCICH

There is something I won't forgive the man, and I ask myself what. There was nothing more innocent in my life, nothing more delicate, than that strange friendship. On the other hand, although I realized it too late, he and I were accomplices. So much so that my usual lack of scruples aside, I never fell into the temptation of amusing others with the story of our absurd meetings.

It's true that, objectively, there wasn't much to tell. A departure, a return, and between the two legs of the journey, the man stood, suspended. But my perplexity was enormous and that inconclusive wonder, made up of trivialities, passes as usual to my voice, becoming a tale. That summer of '83, drenched in sweat, exhausted from the last gallop, I would dismount at the entrance of my house in Manzanares, unsaddle the horse beneath the pine tree, tie the halter to a branch, pet the long, strong-smelling neck of a surly black horse I had, cross the garden as if in a dream, greet everyone, tear off my boots in the patio, enter the house hurriedly, go into the bathroom, and, like a drunk, half undressed, with unjustifiable shame, I would submerge myself under the shower's startling torrent. Later (much later) I would go to lunch and the siesta, the red of sunset would descend unto the grass, the sky would open up deep and black. And all the while not uttering a word.

The first meeting was at the turn to Santa Coloma, one Sunday morning, so early that that ardent summer's air retained the precarious freshness picked up throughout the countryside during the night, and it shouldn't have happened: I was galloping toward Fatima, and the man, his back to the road, was already pulling out his watch and giving it a bitter and furtive glance. A distance of about two hundred meters of flat land and an abyss of mutual ignorance separated us.

It was a solitary place, an artificial desert, made so by early rising. That desolation had the charm of an ephemeral existence. One knew that the apparent vastness of those small fields was a simple artifice of lights and shadows, of precarious colors like the budding and moribund pink, like the faded purple, and that the silence of the plain was only the echo of a breath, the pounding of the black horse's hooves while everyone slept. That illusion of freedom and abandon lasted only as long as the sun's implacable march from the east; it evaporated with the dew and in a moment of realistic enchantment I had the truth before me: towns, farms, country estates, the short route to Buenos Aires.

That moment hadn't arrived, as I was galloping in the emptiness toward a line of horizons that assembled themselves like doors of light in an interminable hallway; I was about to cross the railroad tracks on which I never saw a train, when my horse became frightened. By its shadow reflected in a puddle, by shimmerings on the tracks partly covered by the weeds, the reason for it doesn't matter much. It was a nervous horse, easily frightened. When I was able to regain control of it, we were already on the left-hand side of the turnoff road.

I saw the car before I saw the man. I saw it as one sees things from on top a nervous horse. It was a large car, red, shining dangerously against the yellow plain behind it, in the brown crest of the tracks left by tractors. I wondered if the horse could pass through, and held myself tightly in the stirrups, squeezed the whip's handle, ready to fight it. It passed through with a long stride.

Overwhelmed by the heat, tense with fury because the horse had spent its rancor on the road to Fatima and now floated, with Olympic elegance, on the road to Santa Coloma, I had only a fleeting glimpse of the man. A gray suit, a light blue shirt, a very pale face. I didn't turn to look at him. He gave no sign of having seen me.

I was galloping away, loosening my body on the saddle, giving myself over to the joy of racing toward nowhere, when I felt a tug of guilt. That man had a problem with his car, nobody to call for help.

The three towns in the area (Manzanares, where I had come from, Fatima, where I was going, Santa Coloma, which I didn't know since my limit was a small woods filled with poplars that lay on the edge of Route Six) were at an unreasonable walking distance, leaving the car behind in that emptiness. There wasn't a soul around, nor would there be any until midmorning. Very rarely on those off-hour outings would I meet a fellow rider or a car. I found the useless wait on the side of the road amusing.

This poor man doesn't know, I said to myself with a tinge of pride, because I did know, how slow the countryside is in rising. But since I do not lack a sense of imposition, that pride in the fear of bothering others, his resignation moved me. I too would not dare knock on the doors of the two nearest houses, which were yet so far away in the heart of their fields, blind and mute beneath the false night of the trees, beneath Sunday's hermetic drowsiness.

The man's patience—he was leaning on the car, his arms crossed, the white face surveying the landscape—made me a bit sorry, a bit uneasy. I halfheartedly pulled on the reins and turned around in a trot. I would offer to deliver a message to the mechanic in Manzanares.

It was strange and very uncomfortable. It took me a few minutes to take in his entire body and only a second of embarrassment and anger to understand that he wasn't waiting for help. The scene lasted an eternity.

The man contemplated the scenery with serene eagerness and an emblematic grin. I wanted to turn back, but I was by then only a step away. He turned his head, startled as if someone had tapped his shoulder on a dark and empty street, saw the horse, probably remembered the previous terror, my brave struggle on the road, concluded I was in danger, and raised a hand, searching for the reins. There was a moment of grotesque confusion. I looked at the car, he looked at the horse. The horse, very still, exhaled sweat and docility; the car was parked.

Face-to-face on the track, in that unfortunate situation that demanded courtesy, there was no choice but to speak to each other.

"Pretty day."

"A bit warm."

The voices, made thinner by the confusion, floated in the air for an instant. The reference to the weather was trivial. It served to suppress the offer to relay a message to the mechanic, to retract the gesture that did not reach the reins, but it did not dissipate the feeling of entrapment in the middle of the emptiness and aggravated the dialogue's incoherence.

"Maybe it will rain tonight because there is a dry spell."

"You think so?"

He discreetly leaned on the car again. He was ceding me a path, still looking at me and smiling, conceding to me the last word. I was playing with the strap of the whip, repaying his kind gesture. We both wanted only one thing: to leave. I to return to my ride, he to return to his focused enjoyment of the scenery. It was impossible to do it abruptly. The error committed, the frustrated impulse to help one another, held us back. Confessing to the error would only lengthen what was an undesirable meeting; not mentioning it paralyzed us. Worse still, it pushed us toward a unique intimacy, that of shipwrecks on our first day on an island.

One of us said:

"It's the time . . ."

It could have been me, and then I must have added:

". . . when the world shows itself most hospitable."

Or it could have been him and then he said:

"It was my father's. It works well. It doesn't run slow, or fast."

He was showing me a watch he had pulled out of his pocket. I took it, stretching over the horse's foamy neck. I saw that it had a spring lid and that the palm of my hand was dirty. The lid popped open and lightly startled me.

"I never carry a watch when I ride. Because of the dirt, it damages it.

"I envy you," he said, and I didn't know what he was referring to.

The man was not young, but at my age (perhaps yours as well) it becomes difficult to translate into numbers the oscillating image of physical features on a person somewhere around the tail end of his or her thirties. There is a day, not fixed on the calendar, when one leaves behind the trusted arithmetic of years and with amazement and undeniable sadness begins to wonder whether the other ghost born between youth and old age is older or younger. Than oneself, of course.

The pallor made him older. A lack of sun, and excessive exhaustion. It was evident that he had not slept. Yet, in spite of the signs of fatigue, that white-skinned face was strong, and the body, although the shoulders tended to hunch over as if to better withstand the weight of a sleepless night, leaned with a relaxation of obedient muscles, a gracile softness against the red, glaring body of the car. The eyes were gray or blue. In any case, light and clear, paying close attention to something they followed in the grass horizon, something invisible in that spot, which the growing light diminished.

"I'm coming from Luján," he said, smiling slightly, as if answering out of politeness a question I had asked. "Or from Azul, who knows. But nothing compares to this place."

From Luján to Azul is three hundred kilometers, from Luján to Manzanares is twenty. And he wasn't sure where he had come from? In my confusion, I agreed:

"The countryside is big."

"Don't let yourself be fooled. It is nowhere near the size of the province of Buenos Aires."

That is when I understood. The suit, the car, the contemplation of the scenery. He was one of the many land buyers from the city searching for a piece of land up for sale. Perhaps he would build a polo field. It was curious: I lost interest. And then, as if we had been released from a spell, everything was set in motion. The horse shook, I held on to the reins, the man pulled out the watch and looked at it with a bitter expression, I raised the whip in salute, said a few more words perhaps, and heard his without paying attention because I was already off at a gallop:

"I would like to stay. But I'm a family man."

I recall my surprise. The surprise came, so to speak, galloping behind me, and caught up to me when I could already make out the first houses of the town. The man was excusing himself for not staying. And it was I, by God, who had left. Adding things up, I could concede to him the formulation of his notions. A family man! With sudden anger, retrospective to boot, I added it up. It pointed to a result that made me burn. An eager woman—not to mention chatty —tempting a responsible man. I felt myself a victim (the impulse to help him which interrupted my ride, the naturalness with which I sustained a dialogue that was so unnatural, my lack of mistrust, all futile) of his vain imagination. The excuse, beyond its vulgarity, so unexpected in the man's good manners, was an insult. A *family man!*

"Fine," I said to myself, laughing as I dismounted, "but there was no hunter, sir. Only a prisoner."

The misunderstanding, while amusing, did not flatter me. On the contrary. It is those trivialities of life, those incidentals, light bitter drops, that prove that one has experience. The man's stupidity showed me that I was not so young as to take it seriously. And I wasn't even offended.

Monday I was in another world and the following Sunday I was again in Manzanares, on horseback at the break of day. But I did not take the road to Fatima but rather the road to the south, the way to Cabred. I would never reach the town, just as I would never reach Fatima or Santa Coloma. I tended to stop right on the edge, at the ambiguous border that separates—with a bridge, a road sign, a hill with eucalyptus—one dream from another. Once the horse rested, I would start back.

I liked the road to Cabred less than the other roads. It had the inconvenience of being the obligatory route for the trucks that pick up the milk from the surrounding farms, as well as being the preferred road for the transport of polo ponies that, dressed like young ladies, their tails braided, go to their elegant martyrdom of running, spurred by blows, their mouths rent, with an air of illusionary pride and nervous indifference. The road did have the advantage of a stream that winds through the fields, crosses under the train tracks, a wooden passage that smells like a century of wood and steel, then it becomes hidden, under a second cement opening (the large bridge) to reappear on the other side, with willows and weeds. That stream was worth a kind of misery of runs cut short by the *Serenísima* truck or the cages of the polo enthusiasts, the stinging eyes caused by the dust raised in their wake. As the horse drank water, I would wet my hands and my face, lie back on the grass, or imagine, with compassionate sympathy, that the marvelous oasis of the *Thousand and One Nights* would not be very different from this humble refuge from Buenos Aires: a bit of clear water, some shade.

That morning, in spite of the time, there was a fog. I am referring to the illusion of dirt suspended in midair, thick and blue, that from a distance looks like a haze of flooded fields. That fictitious fog, rocky, enveloped the stream and the scrub bush on its ravine when I passed it at a gallop. The glimmer of a car stopped a few meters from the bridge also passed by me, like a red rock, rolling out of sight. It explained the fog. A single car could raise clouds of whitish dirt. The only surprising thing was the time. Too early, I told myself, for the milk truck and the trailers carrying polo ponies. It was also too early for the bird hunters, the trout fishermen, the families on picnics.

The wide road to Cabred was deliciously empty. But I didn't go very far on it. My curiosity stopped me. It was difficult for the horse, excited as he was, to obey me. I stopped next to a dried cornfield. I was there for a while, struggling with the horse which resisted stopping, and also with a couple of questions. The wind shook the cornfield, making it rustle. It was a soft rustling, a rattling like the sound of grapeshot fired in the distance. I was afraid, and felt strangely alone. I turned around.

There was a bit of resentment, and a bit of obstinance in my curiosity, because instead of approaching slowly, of spying on it from the road, I kicked the horse with greater impetus than was necessary and we descended at once, in a tangle of wild hay and loosened coarseness, jumping, slipping, until settling firmly—I in the stirrups, the horse on the short grass that carpeted the banks of the stream—a few steps from the man.

This time he looked at me without surprise. He didn't even draw himself back. Unrealistically confident, as if a wall would rise between his body, well dressed in gray, and the black-maned animal carrying a disheveled and dusty woman; he didn't move. He silently lifted his pale face while the light eyes inquired, with the kind irony of a man resigned to accepting others' rude impositions, how he might be of service.

It was the calm desolation of his gaze, indifferent to the horse's excitement, to the woman's interruption, which made me forget that that was my morning, my stream. I thought, I am the intruder, and found myself smiling guiltily at him, an embarrassed smile to which he responded with a forgiving one.

The silence was unbearable. Only the water could be heard, a muffled bubbling. To break the silence, I dismounted. I removed the horse's bit, loosened the cinch, and let the horse go, dragging the halter toward the blurry shore, where it sank its hooves and drank for a long time with that pensive enjoyment common to horses.

When I turned toward the man, who was standing with his hands in his elegant suit's pockets, he seemed so tall to me that I was taken aback. I had forgotten the false sense of one's own height that horses give riders. That moving about as if dragging myself, in front of the man, was very unpleasant, so I sat down on the grass, defiant and ridiculous I suppose, crossing my arms over my knees, my chin turned toward the stream.

"You came earlier today," I said just to say something. My voice sounded like a reproach.

"No, no, at the same time. It is you who arrived earlier."

By God, he was right. The way to Cabred was shorter. I was going to agree, and what was more, amazingly enough, inform him that he interfered with my rides, when he said, sighing deeply:

"How I envy you. You have the countryside right here. It's (pointing to El Estribo, behind the embankment) quite beautiful. Rolling, with hills. And with a stream. I've seen a wooden bridge. A shame for it to fall apart. But on second thought . . . Yes, better that way, impassible, dangerous for cars."

He spoke with nervous inconstancy, going from one observation to another, not very coherent, describing the landscape which we couldn't see because it was walled off by the ravine. The well-mannered, solemn voice, oddly light in spite of its stress—the voice of a person forced to say a few kind words before taking his leave—praised the soft yellow hills, the green fields where a few head of cattle were anchored like boats on a dock. The web of tracks that captured the movement of the countryside, its convulsions of forms, with strong and innocent strings.

"So close," he said, and I saw a voracious flash in the gray eyes, "and it took me so long to discover it."

I listened, engrossed, with pity. Those lands had owners. There wasn't a single meter of paradise for sale. But the idea of disappointing him saddened me. His enthusiasm as a buyer had the serious tone of a boy who asks for the impossible. As all boys, he thought himself unique. Indignant, I asked myself which local broker, guessing his naïveté, had offered him one of those farms intending to then interest him in a house with a mere garden or in a piece of wasteland.

"I was ready to give up." He smiled. "What a coward, I was about to turn back."

Ah, I told myself, that was it. The man had arrived instinctively. He was looking for a nitch for himself. The eternal desire for a soft pillow, a place of one's own, the only place on earth beyond the reach of the world's sorrows. Some are lucky, some aren't. I was the fortunate type, the man was not.

The tracks shook. A railroad cart carrying three men passed as if crossing the sky. The men waved. They went along happily in their toy train.

"I don't have land," I said. "Just a modest weekend house."

"And the horse?"

Like all city people, he believed a horse came with a piece of land attached. The horse, I explained, was just a horse, and was looked after by some country folks from Manzanares. But those fields belonged to me. In some way.

" 'In some way' can be quite a lot." I smiled. "Just look at how the city belongs to us. A street, a plaza, a café. Through the magic of imagination, through the obstinacy of possession. Even a person can belong to us. Why not, then, a handful of fields? Believe me, I am quite a landowner."

"I envy you," he said sadly, and (it seemed to me) with pity.

I felt he was growing distant. He took his eyes off me to fix them, for a moment, on the road to Cabred.

"You envy me because you don't know me," I said, angered by this second mistake, ready to set him straight.

But he wasn't listening to me. Restless, he was turning his head, stretching to see the road. The haze was losing its fake, watery blue, the air was becoming golden, gritty, and I couldn't find the words. The silence, and his inattention, overwhelmed me. I stood up, lifting the bit and the whip off the grass. The man took out his watch, and looked at it with that bitter expression that was already familiar to me. The sound of an engine could be heard in the distance.

"I would like to stay . . ."

Furious, I didn't let him continue.

"That land back there," I said slowly, cruelly, "the one you liked so much, is not for sale. No one in the area is selling. There are only lots. I suggest you go to Cabred. Here . . ."

He looked at me with wonder and a bit alarmed.

"But I don't want to buy anything. I didn't come here to buy. I—" He shook his head, smiled, offensively polite. "Anyway, thank you. You've been very kind."

He agilely climbed the ravine and disappeared from sight.

I crossed the sun and dust on the way back at a furious gallop, crazily, skirting the *Serenísima* truck and inflaming along the way a group of polo ponies. Half blinded, shaking, I stopped in front of the entrance to the house. That visible, extraordinary anger, I had to take out on the horse.

"Always the same," I said. "Temperamental, nervous. I have to sell this horse."

During the week, from time to time, I would remember the man. And not happily. There is a broad superstitious streak in my nature, covered by a broad streak of rationalist pretense, and the memory of the man slid from one to the other, slippery, stubborn, not letting itself be captured by the alarming phantasmagoria of the first nor by the deliberate order of the second. Not even for a moment did I believe his appearances to be none of my business. Reason has its light, though dim and poor, and its fidelity to fact: the man had twice crossed my path, and I didn't want there to be a third. As for his motives, those were his business. *A family man.* And he would look at his watch and go, of course, back to his family. There are men (there are plenty of stories and cartoons of it) who spend the night vagabonding about, looking for another woman, a drink, a friend, to lose themselves, only to find themselves once more, at sunrise, with the same boring and sensible character who protects them from life's uncertainties. This one went to the countryside. So what? But once I was mockingly laughing, I realized it was only awful, nervous laughter.

It's no surprise that the following Sunday, counter to my decision (which was to forget him), counter to my taste (which was to ride on open roads), I would file down Avenida de las Casuarinas toward my last-ditch choice for riding, the entangled woods of the Luján River.

It was dark when I went to the pen where they left my horse for me on Saturday. There were other horses there and I watched them part to the right and left, the *lobunos* silver shadows, the *alzanes* copper ones. As I walked toward mine, I quietly called its name.

The horse raised its splendid head and neighed softly. It knew me, waited for me. At that moment of reunion with no witnesses, at the time when the world is divided in two—a very black starry west, a blue east growing lighter and cloudy—we allowed ourselves a mutual, almost human tenderness. I placed an arm around its neck and for a few silent minutes, my face buried in the soft coat, its thick lips on my shoulder, we remained still in the retreating tide of horses.

But this morning was different from others. It was difficult for me to let go and begin the routine of our little war of wills. This shameful morning we would not run away from the sun but toward it. Because the open roads (Fatima, Cabred, Santa Coloma) lead to the family man with his whim of gazing at landscapes, we would cross through town.

As usual, the dogs of the houses on the Avenida de las Casuarinas—barely a dirt road wider than the others but with those tall trees on either side posing as servants—halfheartedly barked at us, simultaneously pathetic and dignified in their useless loyalty. Then we crossed the section of mixed-up wasteland, of humble homes. An obstinate and compact neighborhood that came unraveled on the way to the river, where the perfume from the minuscule gardens and the mob of animal smells let off by the crowded corrals would become lost in a single whiff of humidity: the smell of a water well exhaled by the hill. There on the shore, in the first arch of black locust trees, skirting the thorns which were long and sharp as knives, I dismounted and led the horse down by the reins through a narrow gauge in the ravine, until reaching the path that wound around the hill. If the hill formed a wall, the river formed a moat. The Sunday cars had to park shyly on the shoulder of the three or four poorly made roads within the confines of the neighborhood. Just as well not to look, I said to myself, and I didn't look. I swear I wasn't thinking of the man. I thought (and my heart jumped) of the astonishment brought about by the abundance of thistle.

A flood of half-dead leaves and fleshy buds erased the path. The small bridge that allowed passage over the river seemed to float and balance itself on that sea of thistle. By comparison, the hill behind it seemed as open as the sky. A sky of branches and blackish thorns. I was weakened by a bout of anguish. There was an affront, a message, in the disappearance of the trail: *Where do you go if the path is removed?* It didn't matter much, actually, since the horse, stepping firmly, plowed through the weeds that reached up to my stirrups with a light, almost joyful, stride. I, on the other hand, was sad.

Seeing him, as I was crossing the bridge, was a relief.

He was walking over the bed of leaves and under the entangled canopy of the old locust trees, slowly, going deeply into the woods as if looking for the site of a greater darkness. More enchanted than surprised, I followed him. I remember the sense of futility that the loose reins in my hand produced. I was being carried on a pedestal toward the figure wandering through the hill, that family man acquired in my recent rides.

My voice sounded terribly strange, like that of a bird, in that solitude without any song.

"Hello."

He didn't answer, just smiled. This time it was a smile of friendship.

"Were you thinking of buying the hill?" I joked nervously.

"Of course not. I hadn't even thought of returning. You know . . ."

And he fell silent. He looked back, the pale mouth tensed, as if, on the verge of confiding in me, he'd been alarmed by the sudden appearance of strangers. We were quite alone, of course. Then he again fixed his light, intelligent, and now calmly happy eyes on me.

"Do you know what paradise is? It's," he said innocently, "the place where one is truly alone, where there is no shame in being alone, and there is no fear or guilt."

I thought of his family and agreed.

"How interesting." The man pointed vaguely to the trees, as if dismissing an error. "The world here is not as big as one imagines."

I know how to place myself in another's shoes. I had a quick vision of the man in the city, the man among the crowded masses, responsibly fulfilling his daily obligations until Saturday, until the moment of escape in search of retreat and peace. Affable, docile, abiding by the judgeless laws that inscribe in stone all living arrangements, he rebelled in his own way. He brought along, trailing behind and because of the lack of time, that urban elegance, that car the color of fresh blood which the dust from the road did not manage to dull, that vigilant watch and the uneasiness of being spotted and followed by the ghosts of his transgression. I imagined him (had I not interrupted him) throwing himself on his knees, ripping apart the impeccable suit on the thorns of the black locust trees, stripping off years, manners, submission, disgust, among the bed of leaves. Night after night he had searched for the meaning of life outside the shapeless and bland mass of his civilized maturity. He had found it. I took pride in the meaning being in my domain, and generously forgot the crossing through the thistle, as if the man, after wrenching my freedom from me, had returned it with renewed strength.

I recall that morning and ask myself if it really happened. The man on foot, I on horseback, approaching one another and separating in a parallel itinerary that shook the low branches and the stray bushes burnt by the lack of water. It was a calm and circular course whose irrationality neither of us perceived. That omission was not accidental. I would translate each word, each gesture, into my own deepest understanding of the man; he, in turn, had already made a decision. We spoke as if in dreams.

I told him I had not set foot on that hill since the summer before last.

"The thistle was here then, but I didn't care. I was on foot, guiding some friends. I had to keep turning back or waiting up for them because I was walking so fast. The thistle scratched my legs and I liked it. Ah, I liked the heat, the lack of air, the mosquitoes."

I sighed and lowered my eyes. The dried leaves crackled and my voice cracked.

"You know, I was happy. Happy beneath the stony sun. I got to the bridge, my friends were left behind. It was only a second. I saw the hill swaying, it was hard to keep my balance. With anguish, in a panic, I understood. That flowering of energy, that flowering of youth with which I crossed the thistle, was just that, a flowering. The deceiving flowers that blossom in the last stretch of summer."

The man was staring at me. Anxiously, I explained.

"It's not pleasant to discover from one second to the next, without prior warning, that something as complex, as immortal as oneself, is trapped inside such a crude machine." I was quiet for a moment, amazed by my vehemence. "It was hard knowing I was getting old."

The gray eyes affably observed me, flatteringly perplexed.

"Does it matter so much?" he asked softly.

I lifted my shoulders.

"No, of course not. I could have turned back. A bit more tired, a bit less agile, bothered by the thistle, complaining about the heat. I didn't turn back. I was frightened, I guess, by the thought of resigning myself to a weakness I feel is not mine. I won't resign myself to it."

"You're doing the right thing," the man said. "I won't either."

A locust branch got in the way, and I lost him in the tangle of trees. When another clearing drew us together, I saw he was still smiling.

"My God," he said, facing me. He had the tone, half teasing, half ashamed, of a friend who, once the secret is out, is embarrassed to have told it. "You and I are accomplices in a rebellion so subtle against a condition so vague, we are like two pitiful flies trapped in a single spiderweb. As for myself . . ."

I thought there was more to this than a family man's situation. And I was willing to listen to the old story.

"My God," he repeated, this time in a pained tone.

I thought he was overstating a family man's situation. And prepared myself to listen to the same old story.

"My God," he repeated, this time with a painful note.

He didn't say another word.

We retraced our steps in silence. I was impressed by his dignity. Only much later (the ride through the hill became longer) did he say:

"We coincided, it's true. But with one difference. I wove my own spiderweb."

The man didn't know why, didn't remember how. In his memory everything seemed simply sequential, one thing led to another. Yet, there stood the pattern with its geometric figures, a prison crowded with people and suspended in midair, a product of his actions. The desire to escape clashed with the sense of inexcusable responsibility that fit inside the space of the prison he'd built. He found no comfort in taking stock of the mistakes and successes of the past and discovering that a few here and there shared the element of innocence.

"It's enough to live," he said, shuddering, "to, in the space of a few years, turn all innocence into an offense, every impulse into a calculation, the prisoner into the jailer, guarding to maintain order and the welfare of the wretched in his charge."

He raised his head, hesitating.

"I don't know if you understand. I wouldn't be able to break a single thread of that pattern without committing a crime."

"Not a single thread," I said.

"Not one. I've been so fortunate, so happy even, in this senseless existence."

The contradiction should have seemed odd to me. A reasonably happy man does not seek to escape. But I accepted it as natural. There was, in his poise, a certain suffocating order. I noticed for the first time that even in his step through the hill there was a certain order.

He walked between the locust trees as a guest of honor on a carpet which has been especially rolled out, dignified and graceful, elegant but not vain, with the relaxed composure granted by being accustomed to similar homage on similar carpets. It was unthinkable to see him stumble or become blinded by the glare. He didn't even sweat, unlike me, who suddenly, by comparison, found myself dirty and disheveled in my shirt and riding pants, my boots with the leather scratched by the metal in the stirrups. Only the place, the time, the conversation, linked us in a single mess: two romantics and their small adventure.

I already had the story set up (a man in search of his freedom, a woman in search of her youth), I even had the quaint humor that spiced up the meetings of two fools, two incredible nonconformists, spoiled children pretending that the backyard is a jungle, when he stopped walking.

"I want to be alone," he said hoarsely.

I felt annoyance at that voice which was giving an order, and reacted with anger.

"Me too. Or do you think I came here for no reason?"

It was then that the birds let out a hysterical song welcoming the sun. Short, strident, it tore the semidarkness of the shade. The man turned around. That white face, that look of anguish, of supplication, was returning. I said to myself, he is going to look at the watch, I'm going to leave the hill. But he stretched out his hand and dexterously, with a movement so quick that the horse did not manage to become startled, he took the reins from me.

"Wait!"

It wasn't an order. The sweetness in his light eyes had a frightened luster. We were now very close, more joined than separated by the horse. The silence squeezed us together like an additional denseness.

"Excuse me." Very slowly, halfheartedly, he returned the reins. "I didn't mean to offend you."

"For God's sake, you don't have to excuse yourself. How silly."

The meaningless phrases told one story; our faces another. I know mine was burning.

"I must explain myself . . ." he started.

I raised a hand, disdainfully. I hate patriotic speeches and the man was about to give me one.

"Listen," he said. "Please listen."

I don't recall what it was I expected to hear.

"We fell in love," the man said, "the moment we saw each other. It happens sometimes. Even to people like you and me."

I looked at him, astonished. Had he gone mad?

"It's not that big a deal," I said, and thought of love, so miraculous, precariously positioned in the world like the svelte shape of the horse, the silhouette of a man against a backlit background.

He smiled. A malicious smile.

"But we are reasonable people."

"There is something sordid about reasonable people," I interrupted him, indignant. "One more minute and you will tell me about your family and if I'm not careful I'll tell you about mine. If we ever get out of this reasonable conversation on the meaning of life, if we ever get out of this solemn and foolish rumoring."

One of my few attributes is that of making decisions at critical moments. The sun was already reddening the semidarkness. I straightened in the saddle.

"Look, let's assign parcels of land. I'll leave you the hill, you leave me the roads. That way we'll avoid bumping into each other. To each his or her own Eden. You know, we are both searching for the same thing."

"You are mistaken," the man said, very serious.

From on top of the horse he didn't seem so tall. Perhaps during the long, circular stroll, shoulder to shoulder in conversation, I had been leaning down to chat with him, because now, sitting up straight,

I felt the difference with a bit of vertigo. Only the light eyes were touching me, their enormous burden, their ironic and bitter expression. For the rest of the man, the only thing remaining was a drop of curiosity, evaporating in my anger. I saw him pull out the watch with clumsy fingers and thought him to be a ridiculous man, a farcical character. The type of coward who enters his own home with his shoes in his hands, shudders and says: *It's late.*

"It's late," he said, and it struck me as so funny that I couldn't help but laugh.

I pictured him in front of his worried family, a tribunal of loved ones who after listening to lies hastily formulated on the way back would absolve him with an embrace and some tears. The man, forgiven, would swear not to go out alone at night ever again, and for a week, as an aside, his gregarious nature would find endless excuses for telling himself that a family man is indeed a lucky man. He wasn't alone and he was loved, each spoke on that wheel of people nailed to his center was a tender and luminous life, according to his or her temperament. But by the eve of the seventh day it was difficult to tell them apart, and forced to watch them roll, felt only nausea in the face of that round thing that spun around and around, then he would get in the car, looking for a few meters of undeveloped and firm land where he could sink his feet.

"I don't think we'll see each other again," the man said, stroking my horse's mane.

With the same gentleness, with the same distraction, he would stroke his worried wife's damp cheek, a confused young daughter's hair, a sick relative's hand, a bad novel's cover, while remembering to pay the club dues, the parking garage's monthly fee, the light or telephone bills, and look at the watch where he kept, under a gold lid, office hours, lunch meetings, bank appointments, movie schedules, theater schedules, and dates with family friends.

"In that case," he said gravely, "I ask that you understand."

I was about to answer that he wasn't asking for much. Like all men, he liked to think that behind the rough, manly façade lay a sphinx. There was no sphinx. There was only a family and the fear of losing that family. That a dialogue plagued by empty words, by inopportune genuflexions, would make him so uneasy was an insult to my common sense.

"I understand," I said, and because I sensed that my voice revealed some contempt for his domestic spiderweb, I quickly added: "You don't know how well I understand."

What response was he expecting? What erroneous emotion had I communicated? He looked at me confused. He had a dumb air about him with those eyes full of amazement, that half-open mouth. He remained that way for a moment, contemplating me from the depths of his inexplicable stupor. I said to myself, he is fighting back an impulse to tell me a private story with its miserable details.

Once again his dignity prevailed. Perhaps fed up with providing explanations, he shook his head and smiled ironically.

"No, my dear friend. You don't understand."

By then, in spite of my low self-esteem, I was starting to feel insulted. More so than the man and his strange talent in transforming a glass of water into a raging sea, what suffocated me was the absurdity of my position, the alarming suspicion that I was dragging myself into his labyrinth of errors. And I turned to leave the hill.

"What's on the other side?"

The question jumped out at me. I swear I was almost off the hill, like a person dreams he or she is almost out of the dream. The man was real.

"The other side?"

Without being aware of it, I must have given the horse a kick, because a few meters of the bed of leaves and a thorny branch distanced us from each other. Tall, thin, pale, the man pointed toward the west. I didn't see anything ridiculous, anything contemptible in that figure. He was an attractive man. That until that moment I hadn't been able to perceive what was obvious proves the destiny of simple truths. I only confess that the man pained me.

Without bitterness, I saw that his recently outlined territory worried him. He had a will less malleable than my own.

"There is nothing," I said. "They wanted to build a country club there."

They were very low-lying lands. To the west and the south they bordered the hill and the river and were easily flooded. From the pine tree in front of the house, while I unsaddled the horse, that deserted landscape hung before the entrance of the house like an old calendar with an illustration of the *pampa*. In the days of initial enthusiasm, they had dammed the stream, and the man-made lake—where the stream in its death throes continued to pull up rusty drainage—would overflow with the rain, making the fields a straw-dotted sea. I would look at that land from on top the black horse as an illusion. One morning it would disappear under a current of houses, under a flood of families.

"Until now they haven't sold a single lot. Sometimes somebody goes to fish in the lake, but the floods of drainage do more to hold people back than the wire fencing. Rest assured, nobody cares much for the place."

The man looked pensively toward the west. Because he inspired pity, I added:

"The only entrance to it is across from my house. It has a gate. Cars can't get through. Nor horses."

I should have left then. I didn't. I recognize in myself an uncertain inclination toward theatrical gestures.

"Friends?"

"But of course!"

I had the impression that had I told him my name he would not have remembered it. That impression must have been reflected on my face, because the smile dissolved.

It is difficult for me to describe the slow ascent of his melancholy. Another man made his way through the happy facial expressions, like a solitary explorer makes his way through the jungle. That other man said, with the saddest eyes in the world:

"It's late, dear."

I looked at my bare wrist and agreed. In silence, I let go of the man's hand.

As I galloped on the Avenida de las Casuarinas, I imagined him walking toward the secretly parked car, then on the way to Buenos Aires repeating *It's late*, and I felt so sorry, so tired by the time, the heat, the summer, that that night, when it finally came after an interminable day, I woke up startled and found it empty. I don't know if I felt relief. I felt that sense of the surreal that punishes the inventor of tales once the story is over, the pact with her character closed. We wouldn't see each other again.

But we did see each other, that same Monday, in the middle of Calle Florida, for a few seconds frozen by our amazement.

Neither one of us was alone (fate is a clumsy magician) and we were walking in opposite directions. Had it been otherwise, perhaps, leaping over the wall of modesty, of timidity, of plain tameness in the face of such circumstances, we would have stopped, we would have talked, and then . . . Who knows. In any case, we kept on walking and took a while to recognize each other. This is not hard to believe.

A few seconds before crossing paths, I saw in the crowd, fleetingly, like a playing card in a tarot deck, a tall and elegant figure, a well-constructed face, very light eyes that shone happily, a smile on the verge of laughter, and thought: That is one happy man. And what had he seen? A woman in a summer dress, with books tucked under her arm and a certain desire to wander out which a long day in front of the typewriter produces. A river of people stood between us and we were able only to share a vague sense of surprise, a quiet sense of alarm.

"Who was that?"

"What?"

"The man who greeted you."

So we had greeted each other. A reflex of a politeness so efficiently ingrained that it, on its own, ordered the movement of muscles. But my thoughts, my emotions, were elsewhere. They were sixty kilometers away, on the road to Cabred, on the shore of the stream in Manzanares, on the hill filled with locust trees.

"I don't know," I said, and I wasn't lying.

But there was something in the glances the man and I had exchanged that made it seem otherwise. All secrets are concealable; complicity rarely is.

"A family man," I said.

It sounded implausible, even to me.

Immediately after those three words were uttered, I realized I was shielding myself with them to avoid an uncomfortable answer. *A family man*. With that phrase reduced to nil in significance, the man refused to tell his truth; I, to tell mine. What was the truth? That the man didn't actually have a family. As for me, those wild races with the black horse, those furtive rides, were nothing more than the evidence of my still-painful youth.

I would be exaggerating if I said I thought of the man often that week. No. I would forget him quickly, with the help of laziness, of a routine, and the good fortune of that basic resignation that comes with the biggest disappointments. Only now and then, like the memory of some meaningful event that took place long before, I was overtaken by pangs of nostalgia. For that brief moment the man was engulfed by a shadow. It was the shadow of a mistake.

Sunday morning that shadow grew as I clumsily saddled the

horse, incorrectly knotted the cinch, repeatedly misplaced the whip, and finally mounted somehow—the horse was worse than ever—and I set out toward Fatima. At the moment I was crossing the railroad tracks, a metallic reflection to my left, on the turn to Santa Coloma, made my heart skip a beat. I stopped the horse so violently that I almost went sailing over its head. And the car that had been stopped started up.

It was a medium-size black car. I was still blinking, half blind in the cloud of dust and tightly holding back the black horse which, all nervous, wanted to run off, when the car disappeared from the shoulder.

I confess that my excitement horrified me. I lowered my head, confronted as I was by the always vicious evidence, always useless as well, of the narrow channel where our imaginations overturn. A single car, by not being large and red, managed to accomplish what neither a surly horse, nor my inexperience as a rider, nor the blandness of habit, had been able to do until that sad morning: How short the road seemed, how small the countryside, the world. Everything was stuck to the asphalt. In a couple of minutes I reached the hill crowded with poplars. I didn't even dismount.

There was time to spare, and as the country folks said, I had horse to spare.

At a fierce gallop on the way to Cabred, even though it was too early for the *Serenísima* truck or the trailer of polo ponies, I passed a dust cloud and (for the first time in so many early mornings of imprudent racing) I was scared of the horse. In a moment of anguish I pulled on the reins with all my might to no avail. It wouldn't have surprised me if it bolted out of control. It started to run; it deserved another rider. Drunk on speed and panic, I let it go until exhaustion would resolve the battle in favor of one or the other. Something disgusted me and it wasn't my impotence, my body loose and shaky, clumsily holding on to that magnificent animal in flight, biting into the dust that was entering my mouth. It was disgust with my resignation. There was an abyss of pleasure in letting myself fall, pleasure in the anticipation of the end, which freed me of all danger, of all the miserable cunning employed in avoiding it. I thought—if I was thinking at all—that the horse was following his own temperament and, more secretly, my own. Both seemed admirable and stupid, like the heroes in a puppet show.

But the horse had some sense of acquired responsibilities, a memory of its cargo, a soul. Without the mediation of a strong pull on the reins, a lashing from the whip, or a single word, it stopped, with an almost human sense of astonishment, after we crossed the bridge. I managed to see that a car, like a black stone, rolled away and became lost on the road to Cabred.

I went down to the stream very slowly, exhausted, my mouth dry and breathless. The sun was high. There were scraps of plastic in the water, cans and empty bottles on the shore. How poor and dirty, this true oasis. From on top of the horse, soaked in sweat, I looked at the landscape. It had no other beauty than its precarious desolation and, without the man, it made no sense.

"What are you doing in Buenos Aires," I asked, hurt, "while I am here?"

It was then that, dismayed, I discovered the truth. My truth, at least. There is no nightmare as terrible as that of finding and losing something vital.

For the last time in Manzanares, for the last time in my life, I gave the horse a light kick and ran an honest and crazy race. I was going toward the man. I was going to ask for a new beginning. I ran without seeing the birds from which the inexistent avenue took its name. The tourists who were already setting out on their excursion to the river, I left them behind like the residue of a bad dream. I descended with a single leap at the arch formed by locust trees, and crossed the thistle on foot. The scratches didn't bother me, nor the heat, nor the mosquitoes. Behind it, the shadows parted, the man would be there, waiting for me.

It was late.

As I was heading back at a trot on the Avenida de las Casuarinas, I recalled the handsome pale face, the ironic and sad eyes, the sickened voice that had said *it's late*, and I felt so sorry for him, so sorry for myself, felt such shame for the solitude that arms made-up stories, such bitterness for not having understood him, that when I reached the house and saw all of those people gathered in front of the gate to the country club, I didn't look. I knew what they were looking at. A dead man.

In silence, I began to unsaddle the horse beneath the pine tree. The black horse and the harness were edged with foam. An ambulance howled around the corner and neither I nor the horse moved.

"Did you see how strange?" my family, peering out to the street, commented. "That man came to Manzanares to shoot himself."

A black car passed in front of the house.

"That's his family," they said.

"Who knows," I said.

And I still have my doubts.

Translated by Delia Poey

Bottles

ALCINA LUBITCH
DOMECQ

Mom was taken away, I don't know exactly where. Dad says she is in a nice place where they take good care of her. I miss her . . . although I understand. Dad says she suffered from a sickening love for bottles. First she started to buy them in the supermarket. All sorts of bottles—plastic and crystal, big and small. Everything had to be packed in a bottle—noodle soup, lemon juice, bathroom soap, pencils. She just wouldn't buy something that wasn't in one. Dad complained. Sometimes that was the reason we wouldn't have toilet paper, or there wouldn't be any salt. And Mom used to kiss the bottles all day long. She polished them with great affection, talked to them, and at times I remember her saying she was going to eat one. You could open a kitchen cabinet and find a million bottles. A million. I hated them, and so did my sister. I mean, why store the dirty linen in a huge bottle the size of a garbage can? Dad says Mom didn't know anything about logic. I remember one night, after dinner, when Mom apologized and left in a hurry. An hour later she returned with a box full of wine bottles. Dad asked her what had gotten into her. She said she had been at the liquor store, and immediately started to empty every single bottle into the toilet. All the wine was dumped. She needed just the bottles. Dad and I and my sister merely sat there, on the living room couch, watching Mom wash and kiss those ugly wine bottles. I think my sister began to cry. But Mom didn't care. Then Dad called the police, but they didn't do a thing. Weeks later, we pretended to have forgotten everything. It was then that Mom began screaming that she was pregnant, like when my sister was born. She was shouting that a tiny plastic bottle was living inside her stomach. She said she was having pain. She was vomiting and pale. She cried a lot. Dad called an ambulance and Mom was taken to the hospital. There the doctors took X rays and checked her all over. Nothing was wrong. They just couldn't find the tiny plastic bottle. But for days she kept insisting that it was living inside her, growing; that's what she used to say to me and my sister. Not to Dad anymore, because he wouldn't listen to her, he just wouldn't listen. I miss Mom. . . . She was taken away a month later, after the event with the statue in the living room. You see, one afternoon she decided that the tiny bottle wasn't in her stomach anymore. Now she felt bad because something was going to happen to her. Like a prophecy. She was feeling that something was coming upon her. And next morning, before my sister and I left for school, we found Mom near the couch, standing in the living room. She was vertical, standing straight. She couldn't walk around. Like in a cell. I asked her why she wouldn't move, why she wouldn't go to the kitchen or to my room. Mom answered that she couldn't because she was trapped in a bottle, a gigantic one. We could see her, and she could see us too, but according to Mom, nobody could touch her body because there was glass surrounding it. Actually, I touched her and I never felt any glass. Neither did Dad or my sister. But she insisted that she couldn't feel us. For days she stayed in that position, and after some time I was able to picture the big bottle. Mom was like a spider you catch in the backyard and suffocate in Tupperware. That's when the ambulance came for the second time. I wasn't home, but Dad was. He was there when they took her away. I was at school, although I knew what was happening. That same day we threw away all the bottles in a nearby dump. The neighbors were staring at us but we didn't care. It felt good, very good.

Translated by Ilan Stavans

Aunt Elvira

ANGELES MASTRETTA

As a girl, Aunt Elvira was scared of the dark. Her sisters believed it was because nothing could be seen in the darkness, but the reason for her fear was exactly the opposite: in the dark she saw everything. From the darkness came spiders and gigantic vampires, out came her mother in a nightgown embracing a crucifix, out came her father on all fours, contemplating a green comet, her grandfather and uncles hurriedly stumbled over him, opening their purple mouths to howl without anyone hearing them. In the dark there was a girl tied to the staircase railing by a satin ribbon that drew blood. Aunt Elvira said nothing, but she moved her lips as if saying "There are lions and birds floating dead in their fish tanks."

"Don't make things up, Elvira," her sisters told her. "There is nothing in the dark except what is there when there is light."

Yet even in the light Aunt Elvira did not see the same things as her sisters. She was capable of converting the piano into a lizard, the pantry into Ali Baba's cave, the fountain into the Black Sea, and the *Rosa de Jamaica* drink into the blood of the executed.

They said Aunt Elvira was always a bit out of touch with reality, but in the time she dedicated to it she learned how to embroider just as any other respectable young woman, to play the piano without beating the keys, to sing all the decent songs, including the nine most beautiful versions of the "Ave María."

She could cook everything except cod. Her maternal grandmother had been adamant in keeping her daughters and granddaughters from learning the preparation of that dish because in Spain it was peasant food, and if she had gone to so much trouble to live in Mexico, it wasn't so that her decendants would wind up eating dried fish, like some poverty-stricken Andalusian.

Aunt Elvira had her mother's black eyes and her father's impudent mouth. A talkative and articulate mouth without which she would have been able to marry before twenty years of age any Creole with fifty generations behind him, or one of those Spaniards recently delivered from poverty, who had fared well in America. Or in the case of an inevitable love, and given that her father practiced a racial tolerance that was actually indifference, some hardworking and astute Lebanese. Any of these men expected, like all others, to settle down with a woman who wouldn't be giving opinions, or meddling in men's conversations, or positing solutions for the collection and disposal of waste or the current epidemic afflicting governors. Women were not meant to discuss topics other than the domestic, and the less they talked, the better. Women were to sew and sing, to cook and pray, to sleep and wake when it was proper to do so.

It was known throughout the city that Aunt Elvira Almada was not only more full of opinions than an editorial page, but also had strange habits. Some as strange as staying up until three o'clock in the morning and not being able to wake up in time even for nine o'clock Mass, which was the last one. At nine and at ten o'clock Aunt Elvira slept like the baby nobody would make under her navel precisely because she didn't care where she had to have her navel at any given moment. In those days, the ladies were very careful to take their navels to eight o'clock Mass and return home with them as soon as it was over so that nobody would think they were strolling about like busybodies. From then until it was time for the midday meal, they cooked or did some gardening, helped their mothers or wrote chaste letters to practice to the point of perfection their cursive handwriting. The more restless gossiped or memorized a tearful poem.

By contrast, Aunt Elvira and her navel awakened at around eleven. They spent the morning reading novels and social theories, until a fierce hunger overcame the navel, signaling the time to give oneself over to the use of pitchers and basins so as to bathe the entire body in a scattered yet fastidious manner. First the space between her legs, with its little hairs, in which the idea of a lice acquired from some corner during the course of the night was horrific; then the armpits, from which she removed the hair with the same obstinate attitude as a present-day woman; then the navel, and finally the feet and knees. Once well bathed, she applied rose lotion to the ten points she considered cardinal and placed beet coloring on her cheeks. She performed this last task with such skill and had done so from such a tender age that even her mother was certain that her daughter Elvira possessed a splendid natural glow. She was always the last to arrive in the dining room, but was always on time.

"Good morning, sweetheart," said her mother, who lived in agony over the behavior of that piece of her standing before her, like everyone, destined to solitude.

"Good morning," she replied with the peaceful soul of one who rises for breakfast at six in the morning. Lunch was always her first meal, and even though destiny had placed her in unlucky and morningless days , she was never able to eat before two-thirty in the afternoon. That was the time of her father's daily return from completing business deals and failures.

Aunt Elvira liked to guide the conversation in that direction. Her father's world was full of projects and illusions and she enjoyed trying to get everyone in the family to sail along. There wasn't a dead-end deal her father wouldn't undertake. He had bought a factory in bankruptcy for the price of a new one, and it owed in back taxes more than it had cost. The governor ended up declaring that it be given over to the workers, and Elvira's father accepted the decision without complaint. With what was left over, he bought stock in a salt mine that was actually a company set up by two failed geniuses attempting to desalinize seawater. He later imported German and Chinese dishware. In order to sell it, he opened a gift shop that soon turned into the most popular gathering place in the city. There was always coffee and cigarettes for anyone who manifested the slightest interest in the purchase or use of the porcelain.

One year after the opening, the business went under and was

forced to close, but the people had grown so accustomed to spending hours there, drinking coffee and gossiping, that the Turk who bought it and converted it to a taco restaurant became rich under the very nose of the good Don José Antonio Almada.

In the face of such disappointment, Mr. Almada traveled all the way to Guerrero in search of land and returned the owner of property that stretched along the coast in a port called Acapulco, which according to him would turn into one of the most famous beaches in the world. That time his wife intervened and she, who would never have dared to mention such a word, threatened divorce if her husband would not immediately sell the five hectares of that inhospitable beach. Such being the case, Elvira's father sold his beach and lost what would have been the only profitable venture of his life.

"Something bad will come of this," he said the day his land was sold. "One can't disparage such a marvel without paying a price."

With all his enterpreneurial fantasies exhausted, Mr. Almada entered politics with the same vehemence and ignorance he had brought to the business world. As if it wasn't common knowledge that it was best not to cross paths with the government, Aunt Elvira's father thought it wise to dust off his law practice by defending a bullfighter who had been unable to collect payment from the governor for his work in the bull ring, during which he confronted six beasts with unfiled horns, and performed one fight after the other in honor of the heroes of Cinco de Mayo.

To Aunt Elvira's father, who watched the bullfight with the same devotion as others attend Mass or go to the bank, it seemed too much to bear. It was one thing for the governor to carry the authority of his investiture to the point of managing public finances as if they were his own, and another to calmly deny an artist his salary because he had not killed the last bull on the first attempt.

"Here the circus is free," the governor told him. "I can give you bread and a woman, but don't even dream of money. Furthermore, you behaved like a butcher."

The bullfighter had proven his valor during three consecutive hours and was unable to contain himself. He called the governor a tyrant, a murderer, and a thief. The governor responded by having him jailed.

Aunt Elvira's father wasted no time in starting out toward the jail to offer the bullfighter his services.

He filed suit against the government leader, charging him with theft and abuse of power. By lunchtime he was almost certain he would win the lawsuit. He had recruited the help of friends in the press, who owed him so much coffee and considered the charges to be of tolerable magnitude to hold against the governor. They dedicated lengthy prose to doubting that a man as magnanimous and impassioned by bullfighting as the governor could have possibly mistreated a bullfighter. It was surely not that way at all, but if there had been some misunderstanding, here was that honorable man named José Antonio Almada.

They were having dessert when an assistant arrived with the message that the bullfighter was going to be freed. Aunt Elvira took three spoonfuls of her custard and left running after her father. They arrived in time to witness the signature of release and her father's pleasure was such that he took Aunt Elvira to a cantina where little by little revelers arrived. What ensued was a party of brandy and anisettes, music and debauchery from the likes of which Aunt Elvira Almada's reputation never recovered. She had danced with the bull-fighter until both fell upon a table, exhausted. She had drunk *chinchón* and used men's words with such shamelessness and skill that all those present forgot that one of the respectable young ladies of the Almada family was among them. They did not remember that she was she until the following morning. At that time, Elvira and her father returned home singing and slurring "Estrellita" and declaring their love.

"Listen carefully, girl," her father said. "I am the only man in your life who will love you without asking anything in return."

"And I the only woman who will continue to love you when you are old and pee in your pants," Aunt Elvira answered.

They entered the patio, lit by a warm sun, laughing. At its center, standing like a ghost, was Aunt Elvira's mother.

"Do you realize what you've done?" she shouted at her husband.

She was covered by the shawl she wore to church. She had been crying; she couldn't understand what that irresponsible pair had been laughing at. Of course they couldn't realize what they had done. Those who are blissful are blind and deaf as well.

"I got the bullfighter out of jail," the man said. "Did you sleep poorly? You look haggard."

He then kissed his wife cheek to cheek and climbed the stairs thinking only of his pillow.

Aunt Elvira knew that if she remained alone with her mother for one second, the sky could fall on her head, so she ran to the kitchen in search of a quesadilla and a cup of tea . Her mother didn't speak to her nor to her husband for a few days, but she later allowed them both to win her over once again and her demeanor returned to its somber and pleasant state. With the exception of her husband's ineptitude for business, life had been kind to Aunt Elvira's mother. But her short imagination led her to firmly believe the Salesian version of the world being evil when it is not good. And Aunt Elvira had a great propensity from a very early age toward a lack of respect for what everyone considered good.

Just as people had guessed, it hadn't been Mr. Almada's legal and journalistic maneuvering that had freed the bullfighter, but rather the simple fact that the governor recalled with pleasure, the day following the bullfight, the man's moments of bravery. His mood thus uplifted, he considered it an injustice to keep the man jailed for merely extending his courage to a confrontation with the governor. He even had the bullfighter given full payment and the two men eventually came to share something that would be difficult to term friendship, but which nevertheless resembled it.

In the end, as in all his business ventures, the one who ended up without a leg to stand on was Aunt Elvira's father, who, of course, never found out the truth. That is why shortly thereafter he became enthusiastically involved with the case of a group of workers on strike, whom the government had ordered to peacefully return to work, which simply meant to return without a single gain. Salaries and benefits be damned; the important thing was to reestablish productivity.

As if he actually had to be coaxed into taking up that cause with a passion, the final push for Aunt Elvira's father came in the form of the statement regarding productivity. No good person could forcefully be required to be productive, and much less determine that others should be so. He made statements in the newspapers against those who would assume productivity to be the sole criterion used to judge human beings, seizing the opportunity to criticize those whose only goal in life is the search for power and money, and once again launched a campaign against the governor and his allies.

All of this, when said at home or with his friends, won him praise and admiration. But put in ink on paper, it sounded like madness, suicide, the worst venture that José Antonio Almada would undertake in the course of his warm and generous existence.

The story of the celebration with the bullfighter had reached the governor. The person who had related it to him had described Aunt Elvira as a jewel of passion and beauty that had shone that night.

"To each where it hurts," said the governor, consumed with laughter. "And this one makes it easy because he leaves his gravest weakness at liberty. Only a blockhead such as he is capable of something like this."

After the midday meal, Aunt Elvira and her sister Josefina would stroll along La Paz Avenue toward San Juan hill. They were two women who seemed opposites and perhaps this is precisely why they adored each other. Josefina was to marry the city's finest catch, a prudent and wealthy man who, as Aunt Elvira said, would have even been handsome if it weren't for the fact that he always looked as if he was tied up.

Past the halfway point, almost to where the city ended, was the fiancé's house, made even larger by the adjoining flour mill from which came a share of the family fortune. Josefina stopped there so as to spend some time with her mother-in-law, who waited for her at the door and dedicated the following two hours to training the young woman in the exact management and the precise domestic tastes of the family into which she would enter with her gentleness, her intelligence, and her perfect waistline.

Aunt Elvira continued along the path alone until reaching the hill, which she climbed with the dexterity of a goat nipping at flower stems, holding on to the grass and the earth with her steady and knowing feet. Upon reaching the top, she would sit back to watch the sunset with the devotion of those familiar with intense prayer. Some *cholulteca* ancestor drove her to that ritual of contemplating the sun and the volcanoes.

From that ceremony she was one day kidnapped. She was blindfolded and taken down the side of the hill, screaming though nobody could hear. Her sister was two kilometers away, learning delicate embroidery, her mother was baking orange cookies, her father had lit a cigar over a cup of Lebanese coffee and was commenting with his friends upon the misfortune of living in a manichean society such as that of Puebla, which was like that of Mexico, which was ultimately the same as anywhere else.

It wasn't until it got dark that her sister Josefina began to wonder about Aunt Elvira's delay. She was audacious and crazy, but as everyone knew, she didn't like to be in the dark. At first Josefina concealed her distress because she was embarrassed about having to bother her future in-laws by worrying them with the antics of her sister Elvira, who hadn't even waited until after the wedding to get herself into trouble. But when, accompanied by her fiancé and her mother-in-law, she climbed and descended the hill, combing with her eyes the entire area and calling out to her from the car without the slightest response, an uneasy anguish ran from her stomach to her mouth and she stopped speaking. She had to surrender to the certainty that Elvira was not in the surrounding area and return to the house joined to the mill holding back her tears with the expression of a hurt child.

Upon arriving, she found all of her fiancé's family gathered. The father-in-law, the aunts, the sister-in-law, the brother-in-law, and the mother-in-law abandoned their usual discretion and as a gesture of cordiality and good timing began recounting stories of women who had been kidnapped, raped, murdered, and dismembered during the course of the past thirty years. Her mother-in-law had lost in the revolution all the material wealth her husband had accumulated during the same period of time. She blamed the government for each and every one of those barbaric acts, including the little girl who fell down a well when her mother was distracted for only an instant.

José Antonio Almada arrived home at eight o'clock on the dot and found his wife decorating cookies and repeating "The Magnificat" behind a smile. When Mr. Almada asked about the girls, she interrupted her prayer to affirm that they had not returned and the man pounced on her, telling her that she too was nuts, that she couldn't blame Elvira's craziness solely on his side of the family, had she not realized what time it was?

"Yes, I know what time it is," the woman said. "But I didn't make a fuss since I'm always told I exaggerate, so then I'm determined not to scream so as not to seem, how do you put it?"

"Manichean, wife, Manichean. But it's that they never take this long."

"That's what I think. But I've always said that I don't like them walking alone in the evening, Elvira climbing the hill, and it getting dark. And you say I'm being possessive, that that is the way it is in New York, that the twentieth century is well under way and that . . ."

She couldn't go on, and began to cry uncontrollably.

"I'm going to go get them," José Antonio said, trembling.

All afternoon long at the coffeehouse he had heard warnings much graver than those his wife would have ever dared to make regarding the dangers of confronting authority when one had daughters.

He left down the street toward the mill, murmuring improprieties against his daughters who were in all probability there calmly eating *churros*. And against his wife who always ended up being right, and against whose protests he had dared to allow his daughters to be out in the world like human beings and not like the jewels they really were. And also against the bullfighters and the workers on strike, against the governor, and especially against himself.

It was the last cold spell in March and he trembled, resenting it more than any other. When he arrived at the mill, his oldest daughter embraced him as if he too were certain that Aunt Elvira had been lost forever.

Josefina's fiancé came forward to greet him, with the mixture of kindness and perfection that his wife would later detest.

"I know it is imprudent to remind you that I warned you of the dangers of becoming involved in defending workers on strike," he said to Mr. Almada.

"If you know it, then why do you remind me?" Mr. Almada replied, apparently recovering from the initial shock. He had his arm on his daughter Josefina's shoulders, who upon hearing this asked herself if she was choosing a good husband.

Prior to anyone worrying about her, Aunt Elvira had begun to descend the hill with her hands tied and her mouth uncovered. After the initial yelling, she stopped posing any resistance to her kidnapper. Contrary to what he expected, she restrained her throat as soon as she realized that no one would hear her. Ever since she had been told in school the story of Saint Maria Goretti, an adolescent girl who let herself be killed rather than letting herself be taken by a villain, Aunt Elvira had thought that the saint had committed a grave error, and that if at any time her own body were to be in similar danger, she would do everything except stand in opposition to life's plan. So when she found herself trapped by that man with the strong arms and stupid expression, she said:

"If what you want is to take me, I'll go with you. But don't mistreat me."

The man thought it over for a second and then asked her to hold her hands out to tie them.

"Don't cover my mouth because I'll become distressed and faint," Aunt Elvira informed him. "I promise not to scream. But don't worry if I don't keep my promise, there's no one who could hear me anyway."

The man was not as stupid as he looked, and he accepted Elvira's proposition in order not to carry her fainted to the car, where his immediate boss waited, a man in his fifties, flabby and eternally hung over who had made him go up only because, he claimed, he was tired of carrying frightened women.

They began to descend.

"Who do you work for?" Aunt Elvira asked after a while.

"With the Tiger," the young man, who couldn't resist showing off, answered.

"And what does he want with me?" she said.

"How should I know?"

"Are you the type to obey without asking questions?" Aunt Elvira said.

"I heard you were the daughter of some Almada," the young man answered, getting irritated.

"So what? How much do they pay you?"

"A lot. What do you care? It's not like I'm going to support you. I'll take you and leave you there with them."

"Who's going to support me?"

"It depends. You're pretty. Who knows who'll want you. I've seen nothing but pretty ones there."

"You might see them, others do more than just 'see' them," Aunt Elvira said.

The young man came closer, furious; he pinched her arm and kissed her like in the movies.

"This is how you are brave, with the woman tied up?" Aunt Elvira said.

"Did you come alone, or was someone else sent with you?"

"Of course I came with someone else. He's got the car and the gun," the young man said, scanning the bottom of the hill for his friend's car.

There was another car coming down the road, and the old man would have to get farther away so as not to arouse suspicion. That was the plan. If someone was coming, the young man had to hide

Almada's daughter in the small cave that opened up halfway down the hill, on the other side of the path normally used to climb the hill, and exactly where Aunt Elvira and her kidnapper were climbing down. She knew it as well as she knew the entire hill, but she never entered, because it was dark and fetid, full of spiderwebs and mice.

The young man covered Elvira's mouth and dragged her to the cave without experiencing much resistance.

The young woman was as determined as he to get away. She threw herself on the ground, signaled him to do the same, and crawled into the small cave with more speed and agility than the young man. It was getting dark. Aunt Elvira heard Josefina's calls in the distance and felt sorry for her. But she thought that if the Mirandas were to find her tied to an indistinct piece of scum, the life her sister dreamed of in the afternoons would wind up in the garbage without further ado. The shouts finally stopped. The young man looked at Aunt Elvira. Night was upon them, but her body illuminated the growing darkness.

"Why didn't you scream?" he asked her.

"So they wouldn't hurt you," Aunt Elvira answered.

"Damned woman, you want to get me into trouble," he said, coming closer to slowly entice her.

"If I were to steal something, I'd steal it for myself," Aunt Elvira said.

The night had closed in around them, and she felt it would be better to hold on to the idea that she was dreaming. The man kissed her again and rubbed himself against her feverishly.

"Like this, who isn't brave," Aunt Elvira said, dragging herself once again toward the outside of the cave. The man followed her. They felt the air hit their bodies as another caress. He untied her hands and she threw them around his neck. His skin smelled strange. Aunt Elvira thought she had never had so close a skin which was not related to her own. She later closed her eyes and with her free hands touched the stranger as if her fingertips had to commit him to memory. She unbuttoned his shirt little by little until she took it off. Then she covered his eyes with a caress and worked on the belt with such abandon that anyone would guess she had practiced for some time. She went about touching everything and she was skilled and good at it all, right down to the toes which she handled as one who arranges flowers for a centerpiece. She didn't leave the slightest distrust on that body. She placated it by whispering things into the ears and into all of the parts over which her lips passed.

"I knew the rich ones were dumb when it came to this," the young man said in his fervent and passive nakedness.

"We are," Elvira said as she felt his hand moving between her intrepid virgin legs. "We are, we are," she murmured, taking off running like a frightened cat. Leaving behind her the first nude body fate had brought her.

She was hugging the pile of the young man's clothes as she impetuously and desperately ran toward the mill. At the bottom of the hill was a car with the fat man who carried the gun, asleep like the angel he never was. He had returned as soon as the car carrying Josefina and the fiancé had left, and when he saw that his protégé was taking longer than expected, he imagined that something good was going on with him, so he allowed himself a nap. It had seemed right to him to wait until the young man finished his first job, taking a bit of woman from his bosses.

Aunt Elvira passed near the car without turning to look at it. She was propelled by an unknown excitement. What would have happened next? she asked her body for an instant. But instead of answering, it kept running.

She entered the mill with eyes like moons and the mouth of a dead woman. The doorman saw her climb the stairs like a hunted animal. She then entered the living room and embraced her father, who upon seeing her alive felt his heart burst and his body falter.

"All of this was for selling Acapulco," Mr. Almada repeated several times in the dying delirium of the days that followed. "Why did I abandon my business dealings?" he asked everyone who visited him in the hospital.

Aunt Elvira kissed him again and again, her face withered from tears and hopelessness.

"Don't worry, Papa. We'll buy it back, but don't die on me. Don't die."

She continued to beg him not to die well after he was buried, because Aunt Elvira never actually buried her father. She spent the rest of her long life making business deals in his honor. Her mother ceded to her the management of the brick factory in Xonaca, which was the last thing they had left, to see if by making her feel urgently needed she could rescue her from the well into which she had plunged.

And that kept her busy forever. She began by convincing half of the builders in the state that her materials were better made than any others and she ended up the owner of a real salt mine, two of the first five airplanes to ever cross the Mexican sky, three of the first twenty skyscrapers, and four hotels on the Acapulco coast.

"You see, Papa" she would say at the end of her life, every evening in front of the ocean. "We bought back Acapulco."

Translated by Delia Poey

Over
and Over

CARMEN
NARANJO

On the radio they predicted rain for the afternoon with a chance of more in the evening. Doña Juana thought about hanging out the wash after lunch. Doña Lola proposed a game of cards because after all there was nothing better to do. Doña Cristina said she would do her mending; the basketful was starting to weigh on her conscience. The news came on and Doña Josefa proposed saying a rosary for peace in that foreign place over there where thank goodness there are no relatives of ours and people are dying like flies without confession or an act of contrition because bombs fall and scatter them just like that, though who knows whether they have any religion or even believe in God. Doña Susana observed that meat and milk were going up, who knows how much, and what were the poor going to eat now since beans were already sky high and you can't get full chewing on toothpicks, what would become of the poor souls out of work with no homes of their own and a pack of little mouths to feed. Doña Blanca changed the program to the soap opera. Doña Ester confessed she had the feeling all along that this count was good for nothing: "Rosarito, my love, my angel, I love you more than my own lifeblood, I would give you the sun and the moon, cross the darkest forest, kill lions and crocodiles, sell myself into slavery for you, only for you . . ."

And just when he was throwing his arms around her—she was slender as a reed, he was tall and dark with strong hands and broad shoulders—the kettle started to whistle and Doña Toñita got up with a start: Oh my God, I forgot about the cooking! So they didn't find out whether the two of them kissed, and things were bound to get more complicated tomorrow. Doña Estela advised silence and concentration because the same thing always happened, they always lost track right at the most exciting part. Doña Lola got out the cards and started a game of solitaire on a corner of the sofa. The Social Services Department announced with deep sadness the death of Don Esteban Fuentes and extended its condolences to the grieving family; the time of the funeral at the Church of the Immaculate Conception in San Ignacio would be announced as soon as possible. What did he die of, asked Doña Juana. Josefa guessed, they're not from around here, and if he's one of those I'm sure he died of cancer, it's been the same with all of them. Doña Cristina touched wood and kept mending.

At three o'clock it started to rain, a loud and heavy rain. There was no time to bring in the wash. Doña Juana's rheumatism made getting soaked out of the question and the rain was pouring down in sheets with no more warning than what they said on the radio, which you can never trust. "This exercise will work wonders on those spare tires around the tummy; lie flat on the floor and raise your right leg, straighten it, don't bend the knee, rotate in a circle, lower it again and raise the left leg, do the same rotation, and set it down. In time with the music now; one, two, three . . ." Doña Blanca was down on the floor following the instructions. What a spectacle! said Doña Lola, and later you'll be complaining about pains up and down your spine, you're too old to be carrying on like that. The facial exercises began, everyone got up from their chairs. "Keep your head up straight, then let it fall heavily toward the neck, one, two, three . . . Now swing it like a pendulum from your right shoulder to your left, one, two, three . . ." Doña Ester noted the colors of everyone's cheeks, they all looked ten years younger, and Doña Susana brought out a mirror.

The cooking program failed to catch anyone's attention—chile peppers Arabian style. Doña Cristina lost her needle. Doña Josefa argued with Doña Blanca over the exact date of Toñita's wedding anniversary. April 21. March 12. Doña Estela maintained it was June 11, she remembered perfectly, she wore her black shawl with red roses that day for the first time. That shawl was mine, said Doña Juana, I lent it to you for the occasion and it wasn't black, it was light brown with roses of various colors. That was for Jacinto's wedding, Juana, when you wore my Chinese silk scarf, said Doña Susana. Doña Toñita pointed out she was married on the 21st of September, everyone's memory was failing, and after these mnemonic exercises they listened to the latest news: two vehicles destroyed in a traffic accident on 12th Street with nothing but minor injuries. Who was injured? asked Doña Ester. They didn't say, they said only that injuries were minor, Doña Estela explained. These people tell nothing but lies, two cars smashed up and no one dead or wounded, it just isn't possible, no doubt it was people from a good family out getting drunk and that's why they won't give the names, Doña Cristina predicted, I know every trick in the book, and everyone looked at her in reproach as if to say: we don't talk that way here.

As night fell they served coffee while Mexican music played: Doña Estela raised her voice in song for the ballad of Juan Charrasqueado, wearing a faint mustache of coffee, milk, and biscuit crumbs. For "The Weeping Woman" Doña Juana sang bass and Doña Toñita alto. "The Festival of Flowers" drew the whole chorus, but only two sang along with "Guadalajara of the Plains," and by the time "Mexico Lindo" came on, no one was listening at all. Doña Cristina said that Blanca made her First Communion in the school chapel; Doña Lola maintained it was in the Carmelite church, they were living in that neighborhood back then and Father Alberto was the pastor; but it was December, my memory is sharp as a tack, Doña Ester declared, I remember because I wore my pink wool dress, the one that matched the cute little bonnet Grandma embroidered for me, and it was in the chapel of San Antonio. When everyone had taken sides for one version or another, Doña Blanca made it clear that she'd received her First Communion with Manuel, who looked very elegant in a black suit and a white shirt with ruffles on the collar and cuffs; she wore her long linen brocade dress and lace veil crowned with orange blossoms. It was the 15th of March in the church of La Soledad, the fashionable place for high-society First Communion back then. That's it, that's it, said Doña Cristina, clapping her hands, and you were so lovely, I can see you now with your face like an angel, a little sad, it affected you when Juana went away, the first one to go away, poor Juana. And Doña Juana wept for her own going away, a single tear running softly down her blushing left cheek. To tell the truth, Doña Cristina had broken the rules; they never reminded each other of things like that.

On the radio they were announcing which items were marked down at the supermarket and Doña Estela switched the station; life is one big business proposition, she said, there's nothing pure and innocent left, everything's for sale and it's all fraud and deceit. She stopped the dial at the horoscope reading which was already up to Capricorn: Doña Josefa. An inappropriate day for reflecting on the past; concentrate instead on surprises the future may hold. What surprises? said Doña Josefa, there aren't any surprises left for me, everything's over and done with. She smiles as if posing for a portrait. Aquarius followed but no one in the group was Aquarius except for Doña Emilce, who wasn't there yet, maybe later on if God wills it, and strange to say, God wills it when you least think about what He is going to do. A day full of happy experiences, but exercise caution in business. Poor Emilce, so business-minded, Doña Cristina exclaimed, and they all gave her another severe look: this was the third time she'd forgotten the rules. Mentioning those who are absent is totally forbidden; they become restless and disturbed when their names are invoked. The horoscope ended and a sentimental waltz began, dedicated to all the romantic music lovers. Four sat down to play rummy and Doña Lola dealt the cards. Doña Ester half closed her eyes and said she felt dizzy and seasick, but with the feeling that love was about to walk through the door. Doña Susana breathed deeply, as if breath were stirred by the memory of things that never happened and then almost do.

The waltz program ended just as Doña Josefa was asking Doña Toñita to deal her another hand, because all this time she hadn't even had a single pair: with this luck I might as well help with the mending. Doña Toñita observed with a fat person's smiling good humor that maybe the deck was stacked and winning or losing was all the same to her, I play to distract myself and kill time, ha, what an optimist I am, you can't kill time, it's time that kills us. Doña Blanca turned the dial and the news came on again, two bombings, a flood, a campus uprising, a civic campaign, statements by the candidates, the importance of cleanliness, the day's robberies, and then the weddings and social functions. Isn't it something, said Doña Susana, it's always the same, but we still listen to it as if it were news and it really just happened. Turn off the sports, the announcer rubs me the wrong way, Doña Cristina cried out, forgetting that expressions like that were unsuitable. When she felt the corrective glance of all upon her, she shrugged her shoulders and apologized that it was such an effort to learn and adapt but she was trying her best and soon there would be no more mistakes. There were tears in her eyes as she spoke. Doña Juana, kind soul, kissed her on the forehead: "Don't worry, the same thing happened to all of us, I was the first to arrive and what a predicament that was, but after Estela came with so much news and then after all of Susana's suffering it got easier and now we are able to welcome everyone like it's their own home, with the same affection and happiness as ever." Doña Blanca turned off the radio and Doña Ester suggested they turn on the television.

The rain continued, a soft, dull rain. Anyone not looking out the windows or straining to hear the dripping of the tree branches would have said it wasn't raining at all. Doña Toñita insisted on watching the *Heart of the Jungle* series, and they ended up humoring her, even after Doña Lola complained that they always showed the same old trotting giraffes and tapirs running around in circles and herons flying and lions roaring, not to mention the star of the show, that she-ape that repeats the same old thank-you they taught her, over and over. In any case, by the time the elephants and hyenas and ostriches came running, Doña Josefa had stopped nodding off and was sound asleep. So were Doña Estela and Doña Susana. When the film ended with the she-ape clapping her hands, Doña Ester and Doña Juana were the only ones left awake.

Then soup, sandwiches (two for each person, no need to get fat), and tea with saccharine were served. The president's office announced an increase in the price of gasoline. How grand Miguelitio looks! remarked Doña Juana. He's going bald, chided Doña Blanca. Samuel told us he has quite a nagging ulcer and complications will probably set in, said Doña Susana. It doesn't show, he looks so healthy, Doña Toñita concluded. A toothpaste commercial came on and then the main feature, *Serious Business*, about the hijacking of an airplane by two pretty girls. Life isn't worth the trouble, Doña Lola declared, but the others didn't hear her, mesmerized by all the windows shattering from gunfire and the corpse rolling down the stairway. After the girls went off to prison, no longer very pretty now with their hair mussed and dirty, and evil thoughts written all over their faces, Doña Estela turned off the television. None of the other programs were recommended by the Board of Censors.

They prayed the rosary with the customary devotion, dedicating it patriotically to the betterment of the nation and its many lost souls.

Good night, said Doña Juana after suggesting they leave the door unlocked. She'd had a premonition, a dream that dear Emilce was on her way. It would be just like her to stay outside if she doesn't find a door open, and that would be fatal; you know from experience we arrived suffering colds, some of us even had pneumonia.

Each of them filed off to the bedroom. Doña Lola took the radio since she liked listening to the political talk shows. Doña Ester left a nightgown and a bathrobe in the entrance; Emilce was so vain she'd want to change right away. They never talked about it but they preferred newcomers to arrive in the morning or afternoon, not at night. That was definitely better; they could smile and endure the weeping and shouting more calmly then.

Doña Emilce arrived that night at eleven o'clock. She came in through the open door and shouted when she tripped over the sofa. She carried her head in her hands like a trophy, and the head cried out when it saw Doña Juana, who came running in to receive her with open arms, welcome! welcome!, calling for Doña Cristina that there was some mending to do. Doña Estela sat Doña Emilce down, practically by force, and in the tussle, the head rolled onto the rug. Doña Blanca lifted it carefully, closed its eyes, and made the sign of the cross over it. Between Doña Ester and Doña Toñita they managed to position it on her neck while the others held down the shoulders, legs, and trunk which were shaking from her moans and cries: I don't want to be here, I don't want to be here. Finally Doña Cristina found the transparent thread and Doña Lola tuned in the radio to the good-night prayer set to religious music: "We thank you for this day, O Lord . . ."

Doña Emilce asked where she was, her face all red from crying and sneezing. No one answered, but they gave her a cup of linden tea and settled her on the sofa with soft pillows and warm sheets and two woolen blankets. The radio announced that an airplane entering the country had been given up for lost near the harbor and a Red Cross rescue team had been dispatched to the area; the passenger list had not been released but apparently it included some very distinguished people.

Calmer now, Doña Emilce said she was hungry but they shouldn't trouble themselves, and Doña Juana went off with a smile to prepare some sandwiches. How nice Juanita is, she hasn't changed, always so motherly and kind. Doña Emilce stared at them all as she said this, amazed at each one's sparkling eyes and tender glances, fresh skin and vibrant hair, soft gestures and kind smiles, their air of peace, and you, Cristina, even you, and she embraced her in tears.

Doña Lola found the midnight concert program too gloomy and switched to the poetry hour sponsored by the Resting Place Funeral Home. "How lovely, oh God, are the dead . . ." Cries of protest drowned out the rhyming singsong voice, which gave way to a program in French on the mysterious life of ants. Doña Lola gave the radio a whack and an old-fashioned tango came on, "with hope in my heart I follow the road of dreams," and Doña Toñita did a zigzagging apache dance across the floor.

Outside, the rain fell like stardust and the scent of roses and carnations was a bracing potion in the darkness.

Doña Estela said that Emilce was barely thirty-seven years old, but Doña Blanca wagered she'd be forty-six next March, while Doña Toñita maintained she'd turned forty-three in August. Doña Juana confessed she couldn't remember, dear little Emilce had grown so, and how pretty she is. The others hastened to agree. With a certain embarrassment Doña Emilce said she would be fifty-one the first of February, and everyone lowered their eyes in silence.

The French program came on again in a burst of static. Another whack yielded the latest news: The minister of commerce was resigning in order to attend to his business affairs. They say he's leaving that job a rich man, Doña Emilce remarked, suddenly coming to life; when he entered the government he didn't have a bed to fall dead on. Doña Juana pointed out that such things were of no interest here; time to sleep, time to sleep, tomorrow is going to be a lovely day and we can sew in the garden under the pretty trees. There are cherry trees here? asked Doña Emilce. And everyone hushed because to tell the truth, Doña Juana couldn't tell a pine tree from a eucalyptus.

Doña Lola tuned in the BBC from London, which was broadcasting *The World Today*, a special program for students of English. Doña Susana said she was getting a nervous headache and didn't want any more noise. Doña Lola complied, and when she tried to turn on the television, Doña Blanca reminded her that by this time of night there was nothing on the air.

A bird fluttered against the window: the first bird of the new day, noted Doña Josefa, and Doña Emilce asked what day and time it was. According to my calculations, said Doña Ester, it's one o'clock in the morning, Monday the 19th of November.

Once again the early bird brushed the window. Doña Cristina, dropping off to sleep, suggested it might be begging for bread crumbs, but no one got up even when the bird pecked at the glass and beat its wings against it. Doña Toñita fell asleep on the shoulder of Doña Ester, who was lying back in the easy chair in the parlor. Doña Emilce and Doña Cristina were asleep on the sofa with their arms around each other. Doña Estela had gone off to bed a while ago, and so had Doña Susana and Doña Blanca. Doña Juana found repose on a bench in the kitchen and Doña Josefa snored rhythmically on the dining room table.

Feeling like an underground revolutionary, Doña Lola tuned in the early-morning philosophy program. She believed—it was true—she secretly believed in the better world of tomorrow.

Translated by Dan Bellm

The Annunciation

CRISTINA PERI ROSSI

I was gathering stones in the water when the Virgin appeared. By the large stones, not the small ones. She came as if from the ocean, although I'm not entirely certain, since the water is very long and very wide, and since I had my head bowed and I was bending over gathering stones. I pick the stones up out of the water, select them, put them in my arms, and take them to the shore. At first, I didn't think it was the Virgin.

The dawn was gray and leaden like an ocean.

I had seen her only once, in church, when we took her out in a procession, I couldn't imagine that I would see her walking toward me along the beach, with that color of eyes and her sorrow due to the death of the son. I couldn't imagine because I am always alone and because she came without a crown, crushing the sand softly beneath her feet. But then, I didn't doubt it for an instant. There is never anyone on this beach, remote and rather distant from the rest of the earth. Separated, isolated, visited only by the sea. I am always alone, gathering stones. At first my hands become frozen and the fingers slip, the fingers that want to grip the stones and fish them out, as if they were marine animals. Whale stones, mountains of the sea. Toward the front, toward the back, and toward the sides, all one sees is waters, green and blue waters, sallow waters, and enormous fixed stones, like boats run aground. I sink my hands in and the fingers slip off the wet surfaces of the stones. The color of the stones is different, depending on whether or not I've taken them out of the water. Sometimes they are full of sea algae and lichens, full of seaweed where the urchins float. But when the hands grow accustomed, they move through the water as if they were fish. I then lean them on the dark surface of the stone, I grip them between my fingers, and I lift them. Hoisted, I take them to the shore.

It's been ten days since we arrived, and since then we haven't seen anybody. Nobody has seen us.

The fishing boats are thrown on the sand, abandoned. On one

of them, wild flowers grow between the corklike planks. Green stems and a white crown among the humid and splintered boards. Slowly it dies. It dies unsteadily, leaning on the sand. A sea gull combs the air, wings outstretched in the shape of a cross, its chest dark, and gently it alights. It perches on the useless oar or the boat, which buries its neck in the sand. Before, when the fishermen went out to sea, on each boat a great lantern was mounted, like an eye that illuminated the intimacies of the waters and the fish. A round eye without lids, with a potent and serene look. The fishermen would clean it, rub it, adjust its light, watch over it. Now the nets hang moldy, and leave their menstrual blood on the sand.

Only a child who plays in the ocean and gathers stones.

Sometimes in the distance a craft passes. The sand invades and climbs over the empty vessels. I gather stones and take them away from the water, so that the waves lapping the shore won't find them. I work this way all morning. I often get tired of hauling stones, my fingers are cold and cramped, the air is green, the trees roar in the wind, the waves howl and there is warning of a commotion, the atmosphere, the elements prepare for something, something is stirring in the ocean's breast, but when I look at the water and see so many stones below, I immediately return to my work, without distractions, without stopping, because at the bottom there are many more. Bent over, the water passes between my legs. The water and a few small fish, silver, agile, and restless. I don't know if they see me. I've never known what and how fish see, nor what they look at, with their large, fixed eyes. I don't know if they part the water to see. If their stares spill over the stones and seaweed on the ocean floor. I was never a fish. Nor have I ever had fins at my sides, I wasn't born in the water, I wasn't nourished by seaweed.

In immense solitude.

There are stones of many colors. I would say: all the colors known and many colors which belong only to water and which only they possess, by living in the ocean, among lichen and plants. If she didn't come out of the water, I don't know where she came from. She wasn't wearing a crown; she walked slowly, as if floating over the sand.

As if he were not alone, as if the water, the stones, and the sound of the wind kept him company. Absolutely concentrated on his task and understanding in some way the harmony of the universe. In that process he discovered his role, his function, and assumed it with dignity and respect, with conviction. Only the sea gulls have been able to see us.

I gather stones every day, even if it rains, or there is wind. Sometimes the sea is still when I go in; still and unmoving like an elephant lying down asleep. The boats do not move and the masts look like crosses. The waters then weigh a lot, as if they were stone. It is solid water, cement water. Nothing moves on the surface; nothing moves inside. The sea is suspended, dense, uniform, heavy. Static, it imprints its serenity on everything; even the birds seem to fly more slowly so as not to skim it. Other times, however, the north wind blows strongly and the sea gulls cannot fly. They are still, in the air, for a long time, their wings tensed and opened, outstretched, but without advancing. They cry and do not move. As if a sting held them captive. And the sea is full of waves, waves that dissolve in the misty atmosphere. Then the boats become restless and want to flee from the storm to the stalls on the beach; there are some which, in their haste to leave, tug on the ropes until they are loosened, and once free, dizzy, like dissolute and wild young women they move from side to side, losing their way, bumping into one another and into the rocks, hitting their hips against the stones. The wind roars, the waves splash against and over the wall, the red buoys sink into the intense ocean and after an instant come up again, poking their heads out like shipwrecked sailors who remain afloat with difficulty, waiting for someone to rescue them. The sea roars and everything seems to be on the brink of breaking: the sky gray and mauve on the brink of breaking into lightning and thunder, the tensed wings of the sea gulls on the brink of breaking, the small wood and stone pier on the brink of breaking, the boats' ropes on the brink of breaking, the lanterns and the masts which lean to one side and another.

How has he come to be here? Who has brought him?

How did she get here? From where did she come? Crossing the sands of beach.

Beneath the sea there are white statues. I have seen them. Sculptured images of women; sometimes they are missing an arm; sometimes a leg; other times, the entire head. They are not always there, they are not always visible. Sometimes the color of the ocean covers them completely; other times, it is the mane of seaweed and its inhabitants, the urchins, which hide their presence. They are so buried at the bottom that they could be confused with it, if the bottom were white, if it had a woman's hips. They never peer above the surface. No current raises them, elevates them, in a pedestal of water. No force from the depths lifts them, hoists them up, like banners. They do not surface to look at the sky, to throw themselves on the sand, like sunbathers. Nothing draws them to the water's exterior. They do not dream of knowing the air, of touching the earth. Sunken at the bottom of the ocean, they sometimes allow a leg to be seen, a white arm, and hide their profile, their delicate hands, their turned neck. They hide their secret shyly, between the pleats of their dresses and distracted fish brush against them, as they pass by, they nibble at their breasts, and lick their white necks. Immensely different from the mutilated cadavers that the sea occasionally drops on the beach, and brings forth from the depths of the war, with terrified eyes and hair stained by seaweed. Pitiful people, it picks them up in silence and without committing itself—they are missing their teeth, their ears, their fingers, their hands—burying them in the pile. Wretched people, in silence it hides them, with them they stone the woods, they pave the earth.

How has he come here? Who has brought him?

I was lifting a stone when I saw her approaching from afar. I did not know then who it was that was coming. The morning was green and the sea was somber. All I saw was a gray figure that came with the wind. The stone was heavy and I had to hold it with both hands. I stole it from the bottom of the ocean when it was still gold; the air darkened it as it emerged and it had, on the surface, small holes where the water had eaten away at it, like multiple eyes that stared at me from within. I placed it on the sand, far from the drilling of the ocean and its grooves, and I returned to the shore, not without first looking—to see that slowly there approached—the gray figure that came with the wind.

Who is the boy?

He comes and goes from the water as if it were his domain. As if only he reigned in all of the area. But humbly. Like a worker. Very concentrated on his task. Without pausing. I think he never rests.

That morning everything was green, gray and green like underwater. Like the color of fish parading among the rocks.

I couldn't turn back because he had seen me. Besides, he was too busy in his task of hauling stones.

I went and came back. I came back and went back out. There were many stones at the bottom; the bottom is always filled with stones and seaweed. She approached slowly. Like the waves, like the wind, she approached, making the sand creak under her feet. She walked slowly without moving her arms, and it seemed that her legs were barely moving. I don't know if she came out of the water or from where she came, because I was very busy with the stones, which give me a lot of work. I only looked forward, I did not look back nor toward the sides.

I was going to continue my path, satisfied that I had not attracted his attention, when suddenly he fixed his eyes on me, as if he had recognized me, as if he had seen me before. He nailed his eyes on me slowly, very slowly, as if identifying me piece by piece, as if his memory were tossing signals to him, fingerprints, he froze, in front of me, now absolutely certain.

I was going to continue my task; I was going to go into the water and bend down, to pick up another stone, when I looked at her. I looked at her closely and recognized her. I was petrified.

I vacillated for an instant.

He was in front of me.

I thought of running. Fleeing.

It is not every day that one sees the Virgin emerging from the water. It is not every day she comes walking along the beach. She didn't appear to be wet and her clothes were completely dry. Her eyes were the color of the ocean which I had seen in church once, when they displayed her to the public and took her for a stroll around town, in a procession. The children and the old people, we carried her like a trophy from the sea. As if she were a giant and very rare fish that would feed us all year long. We took her out of the church and took her for a stroll along the cobblestone streets of the town and everybody came out to see her, the windows swung open and from the balconies the women and children threw flowers, and the old people abandoned their beds and the sick rose to see her and the men who drank standing up, in front of the tin counters, turned their heads, stopped drinking, and respectfully took off their hats to greet her. The entire way I was worried that she would fall from her pedestal—the streets were cobblestones—and roll on the ground. And that her black *Dolorosa* veil would become soiled and that she would lose the beautiful handkerchief she held between her hands to dry her eyes because of the death of her son. I was uneasy the entire way, guarding her path, for fear that she might stumble and fall, and her fine and delicate porcelain hands would get hurt and she would lose her crown and the water of her eyes would spill out.

One time when we caught a very large fish there was also a celebration and a procession and everyone came out to see it and at sunset candles were lit and some made bonfires on the beach. All night long on the open sea the whales snored.

And instead of fleeing I ran toward her, and when I was near I bowed. Ceremoniously, I bowed for an instant. She looked at me serenely; I then raised my head, and saw that her eyes were the color of water. I remembered those eyes well from having seen them during the procession. Sad and undefinable tender eyes. The eyes of a woman whose son has been killed and who feels so much pain that she doesn't think of revenge, because the sorrow is so immense that it calls more for love than for anger. They had killed that woman's son —whose cadaver, perhaps, would still be floating in the water and would appear one of these days on the coast, his throat cut and missing one eye, full of seaweed and lichens, full of lime—and now she was walking along the beach. Long-suffering but she seemed serene. I offered her a bowl made from the bone of a fish in case she wanted to cry, to hold the water. It was a very large fish-bone bowl whose cavity is appropriate for carrying small amounts of water, fruit juices, a woman's tears, and it is also useful for digging in the sand, for making wells. She looked at the bowl and held it in between her hands. The bone becomes white with time, white and dry, with small black markings. She seemed pleased with the gift, but she didn't cry immediately. She held it in her hands for a long time, and looked at herself in it, as if it were a mirror. I immediately began to clean the sand so she could sit down. I chose a square-shaped surface, protected from the sea and the wind by some wild cane. The dunes there rise like mountains and hardly allow one to see the woods. The pyramids are so hard and consistent that nothing can sweep them away, no pounding wind, no rising sea. I cleaned the area with wicker branches, clearing it of ants, insects, pieces of wood, seashells, and residue of the sea. I carefully swept the surface and with my hands, bending down, I leveled it so as to leave it flat and smooth, comfortable to sit on.

I was surprised and wasn't sure what to do. He didn't ask me any questions. He didn't say a single word. He immediately brought me a bowl made of bone and began cleaning the sand, behind a dune, clearing away all dirt and impurities. I looked to one side and then the other, looking for a place where I could disappear.

Then I invited her to sit down. With a gesture I invited her to sit down: I extended my right arm for her to lean on and slowly lower herself, for her to sit on the throne of clean sand that lay next to her. She had the appearance of being tired and of one who knew where she had come from, scouring the shore, suffering, suffering, scouring the shore. Along the way, she had lost her crown or taken it off, since they had killed her son. She had also lost that handkerchief she always carried in her hands, to dry the tears, and the small light-colored dress that covered her body was obviously insufficient for sheltering her from the cold. I invited her to sit down because she seemed tired and the wind was blowing and at any moment the waters would rise, but there she would be protected.

The beach which we all believed to be deserted extended itself toward the front and toward the back. I didn't know this hill, didn't know for certain where the sea ended. I could only turn back, in the midst of exhaustion and cold, turn back, but in the immense empty surface he would have seen me again, had I chosen to turn back. Then, probably, he would have asked me questions. I felt vaguely uneasy, as if awaiting a premonition. The sky, gray and mauve, was suddenly opening, allowing a round sun, of an agonizing color with the shine of metal, to appear. The profiles of a distant woods, completely wrapped in fog, seemed suspended between the sea and the sky, as if levitating. The humid air, palpable, had a stormy tension. The sound of the water as it broke and of the wind approaching seemed to me the death cries of some immense aquatic animal, hidden in the waters. On every side, a revelation seemed to be awaiting.

Once she sat down, I gestured for her to wait, and I took off running toward the hill to look for pine branches, wild flowers, and poppies. I know the hill well, but I was so nervous and excited that I lost time running in useless circles, turns that led me nowhere. Like puppies who leap in the air, twist and turn senselessly when their master comes, I got lost in paths filled with plants, I hurt my hands, I randomly gathered branches and flowers, pulled up roots, nervously crumpled stems, crushed ivy as I walked. And my ears were attuned to the rumbling of the water, they guarded its ascent, its growth, I couldn't see it but I could hear it, like two enemies who know each other well I stalked him and he was willing to take advantage of any carelessness on my part.

I came down from the hill, running, my arms filled with pine branches and wild flowers. I was in such a hurry that I lost a few on the way. She was there, sitting on her patch of sand, protected from the sea, from the wind and the ants, melancholy, looking without seeing, and the breeze ruffled her fragile dress like a boat's sail. One by one I lay the scented branches at her feet, in a circle, careful not to let them touch her dress. There were gray branches with spots of lichens and barks of lighter colors; if I scraped them a little, the true skin of the pine would soon show, green and resinous. There were dry rods, crisp with sharp points, which are used to make fire in the winter. I thought that that aroma would help her cope with the sorrow. She would not look at me, she stared far off into the distance, and the waters of her eyes were deep, like a day of fog and storm. There were a few small pine cones, budding, stuck to the branches, with hard crusts and an intense shine. And between the pine branches, soft and silken like cotton balls, the white starling nests. Tens of lightly woven buds, which the birds embroidered with great care; I thought their light touch and smooth presence would provoke sensations that were amiable, inviting, and warm. Surrounded by branches and plants, by wild flowers and sticks, she looked like a virgin of the hills who had come down to the beach for an instant, to look at the ocean.

Immediately, I went to look for a log shaped like a wolf that the water had dragged in the previous day. Sometimes the water comes like that, bringing things it deposits on the shore, and then leaves, as if it had traveled so far, as if it had gone on for entire days and nights to haul this, to gently push onto the sand the things it gathers on its journey. They are the humble gifts of the sea; after ruminating for hours and hours, after coming and going from the depths to the surface, it tosses a dead fish, a consumed log, a handful of seaweed, or an opened empty shell. They are its humble and humid offerings. It had brought the log the previous day; I found it, not far from there, on the shore, dampened by the waves, and I retrieved it from the water. It took me a great deal of work, because the water it had absorbed made it quite heavy; it had the shape and color of a sea wolf; I grabbed it from the head and sides, dragging it toward the sand. Then I ran to get it. It was now drier, but it was still a wolf; so I grabbed it again from the head and dragged it along the beach until depositing it next to the Virgin. I left it next to her, but facing the ocean, so it wouldn't miss the world from which it had come, in which it had been born and lived. He laid down, tamely, to rest, but kept its head raised, as if assessing the shore and its dangers. Like that, guarded by the figure of the sea wolf, her throne seemed less open, her kingdom better protected. Surrounded by the pine branches, the sticks, and the flowers, having, in front of her, the illustrious figure of the wolf, she looked more like the Virgin I had seen that time in the church, dressed in a black veil and carried in a procession on an ambulatory pedestal. As I had then, this time, I had given her many white flowers, yellow flowers, lilac and blue flowers, pulled from the hill. I came down hurriedly from the woods with them and had one by one placed them on her dress. She sometimes looked back—the dead son—and her eyes were infinitely sad. With a gesture I indicated that the hill was filled with flowers, that there were many more, but I couldn't bring them all, I had other things to do for her. The water advances gravely, step by step, each time closer to us. It left its damp mark on the ground, a bit of foam floated and then retreated, innocently, as if it hadn't advanced, as if it wanted to hide its progress. I looked at the sea and then looked at her. An appreciable distance still separated them, but I nevertheless began to erect a wall of sand, to prevent that a current of water, deviated, wet her feet. I am very fast when I work, and I am accustomed to struggling with the sea. I quickly built a fence of sand, a damp seawall a few centimeters in height to act as a fort against water penetration. I made it that height so that she could look at the ocean, over it, without having to get up, without so much as lifting her head. In turn, this way, the ocean could hardly see her.

He brought me small offerings. Fruits of the sea and the woods. I don't know why he did it, but I thought I could not stop him. Whatever it was he imagined, of which I knew nothing, his gestures were full of kindness and recognition, and I was too tired to refuse those gifts, as misplaced as they were. Immobile, tired, and without strength. But I also thought I could not stay there much longer. Without a doubt it was dangerous to remain out in the open, on the immense beach without defenses, exposed. As dangerous as turning back and having the boy search for me and calling out to find me, alerting anyone of my path. I remained still, not knowing what to do, undecided, more given to exhaustion than to precaution. In the meantime, he would come and go, bringing, in each trip, small presents.

I went to look for a small oar on the beach, half buried in the sand. It had wound up there, the residue of a fishing boat eaten away by salt, humidity, and water, whose skeleton, broken, served as a bastion for some birds. At times I had played inside the boat, in the stagnant water. I had touched its warped wood, its intertwined planks. Felt its crust. Brushed its concavity. And the oar was hidden in the sand, its wider point poking out, useless and bored. I brandished it in the air, like a sword, shaking off the sand that had stuck to it, and with it spinning over my head, I ran through the deserted beach to the dune where the Virgin rested. Happily, I offered it to her, first showing her how to use it. First I made the gestures necessary to navigate. Then, with rapid movements, I showed her how in extreme cases it could be used as a weapon of defense. She didn't pay much attention to my demonstrations. She was preoccupied and insistently looked back. I left the oar at her side, like a queen's scepter. I remembered the well in the rock where I kept the things I rescued from the sea. I was glad to have gathered things every day, which were there now, which I could go and get to give to her. She didn't say anything, but she waited. As a sailor returns after each voyage, loaded with gifts, and happy to be home; as he exhibits, tenderly and complacently, the fabrics from China, the textiles from Holland, the jewels from Egypt; that is how I came and went, intensely, glad to go, glad to return. But her sad eyes looked back, without seeing. Through the entire way, I was afraid she would fall. They chose us, the children and the old people, to take her, to steer her through the multitude, to guide her through the town. I got to push the pedestal from one side. We left the church amid an illustrious and processional silence. Toward the front were the old men and women, toward the back were the children.

We had been in hiding for ten days without anyone seeing us, without any of us being recognized. Only the boy found one of us walking along the beach.

We pushed the cart, which bumped against the stones on the street and shook, stumbling. She was dressed in mourning clothes, with a long black veil, made of velvet, which hung from her head down to her feet, because they had killed her son and she was very sad, a great sorrow came from her eyes the color of water. The veil was black and soft, a very deep black, full of pain. I barely touched the edge of the veil and shuddered. Now she was not dressed in mourning clothes, probably because it had been a long time since the death of her son; it had been a long time but the pain was the same. She was no longer in black, but she suffered just the same. And the hands—the hands which peered out, very dainty and white—under the veil of black velvet held a lace handkerchief, probably to dry the tears when all that water that she carried in her eyes would overflow for the death of her son. The veil had a gold trim, a small pattern of thread which I couldn't summon the courage to touch. She had not yet cried, because the handkerchief was dry, but her expression was of one who could at any moment begin to weep, not with wails, the way the women of the town weep, but rather sadly and tamely, because the tears of one who knows they have killed her only son are not of wailing, but of sorrow. All the torches were lit when we left the church, showing the faces of the old people, full of wrinkles which were deepened by the light of the candles. I was afraid that going over the stones of the streets she would fall.

"She could fall," I told someone from the town, who was pushing alongside me.

"If we walk carefully, she won't fall," he answered, but I was not assured.

If one of the others, for example, was a bit less careful, she could suddenly fall to the ground, and get hurt, and soil the veil, and lose the beautiful handkerchief, and scratch her hands. It was easier between all of us to protect her from the soldiers (from those soldiers who had killed her son) than to prevent her falling.

"Someone might be careless," I said, uneasy.

"She won't fall," he responded. "Between all of us, we'll hold her."

I had put many things in the well in the rock. Old fishing hooks, rusted and still showing their threatening points. Segments of fishing line that had loosened from the rods; pieces of nets that had served to trap fish and had become moldy; large seashells to listen to the ocean, when one is far away and can't see it; a giant fish bone bleached by the sun, a donkey's jaw and many pieces of colored glass, polished by the water. Tree barks with lichens attached, boat's ropes, sailing knots, large twisted nails, and a dark wooden box, which floated in the sea from a sunken boat. I put my hand in the well, and one by one retrieved all the objects. With my hands full I ran to where she was—looking back—and I placed them all on her lap. The sea approached, closer every time, lapping the edge of the sand construction. I dug the fish bone into the top of the wall, like a lookout tower, silent lighthouse, light in the night that warns the navigator of impending danger, sandbar, or sunken ship. At her feet I extended the segment of netting, majestic carpet for her passing; it was a smooth and delicate net; with it I drew the geography of the country in which we would have liked to live, before the war. Around her, like toy towers, like bishops and pawns, I planted the pieces of glass polished by the sea. A mauve-colored horse's head, a steel sword, a golden lantern, a mistletoe cathedral, an emerald fish eye. I placed the knots next to her hair so it wouldn't fly away, to hold it to the sand if it wanted to run, if it wanted to flee, to cry its sorrow somewhere else. And the ropes I tied to her waist, to tie her down, like the boats that are tied to the dock, against the wind and the rocking of the sea. Surrounded by so many trophies, she seemed a sea virgin, a marine sculpture, the figurehead of a ship I had once seen in the Museum of the Sea. With a vine branch I made a crown and placed it on her head. She seemed complete like that, finished and perfect, like the Virgin in the church. Some damp and shiny seaweed, on her dress, made a veil.

He came and went, from the water to the sand, from the sand to me, but always distant, without getting too close. A bird flew and he threw a rock at it. Serious, he brushed away the ants and mollusks. He watched, carefully, the advancement of the waters, and he was always moving, very busy, bringing things.

Then I heard a sound. A different sound, which didn't come from the sea or the sand. I know well the sounds of the beach, the sounds of the birds, of the stirred waters, of the underground currents. I know the sound of the far-off wind, and of the clouds, charged with electricity. I heard a sound and stood up immediately. I looked toward one side and then the other along the beach. The sea, rising, lapped the edge of the wall of sand I had built. The fish bone, erect like a lighthouse, pointed toward the harsh sky. The sea, retreating, left seaweed along the coast. And the sea wolf, lying down, with his head held up, watched, expectantly, close by.

I had to make a decision. Speak to him or flee, return to the place from where I had come, even with the risk that he would follow me, even with the risk that, from afar, he might trace my same path.

The sound was coming from the hill, and was not generated by the trees nor the wind, was not made by the birds or the branches; it was much more muffled and metallic, it was human sound. I stood up on guard; she remained seated, looking back.

"Where are they who killed her son?" I had asked when we took the Virgin out of the church.

"I don't know," a friend answered, "just worry about steering the cart."

For certain they were now looking for her. All that time I had been playing, not worrying about that. All this time lost, without realizing they would be near. I know well the sounds of the sea and the hill. I know when it sounds like a storm, when the wind is approaching, and when the fish rumble. They had crucified him, after making him drag a heavy cross the entire way; they had mocked his pain and would not vacillate in doing it again if they found her. And the water now climbed over the wall, lapping the fish bone.

Then I heard a sound. Not just one, but a prolonged sound and it was followed by others. A sound which filled me with fear and anxiety. I don't know the sounds of the hill and the water well. I always lived in the city.

They were advancing, without a doubt, they were advancing through the hill, and they were firm steps of armed men ready for anything. The steps of the Roman soldiers. They and their heavy swords, and their crowns of thorns and their summary trials, and their slow crucifixions.

The sea gulls cried and the sea swelled. The branches also made sounds as the wind passed through them and I heard breaking, I heard the complaints of logs and the pounding of stones.

I ran to the top of the hill and saw them coming. They carried revolvers and rifles.

Then I made a decision, and began running back, in the direction from which I had come. I started to run and stepped on the flowers, and heard the crushing of the seashells, and a piece of glass cut into my feet. I started to run without looking back, suspicious of the sound of the water, the sound of the wind, and the cries of the birds.

They brought revolvers and rifles, dogs, knives, and lanterns. From the top of the hill I saw them coming. There were many Roman soldiers and their functionaries, their employees, their vassals and servants.

I ran without thinking, ran without knowing, I ran through the waters, the birds, and the wind. Then I saw him. He was holding up two large wooden oars which he spun above his head, to scare off the soldiers. He probably thrust himself on them by surprise, protected by the shadows of the sunset. He knocked down two or three that way, running with the oars in his hands and waving them like the blades of a windmill. At first he must have caused confusion. It was dark and he was very agile. He moved with great speed, from one side to the other, without letting go of the oars.

I ran without thinking, ran without knowing, ran through the waters, the birds, and the wind, to stop them.

But then I saw nothing more. I had to turn my head, to keep running. Until I recognized the sound of the gunshots. The only sound which is heard in the city.

Translated by Delia Poey

The Rupture

ELENA
PONIATOWSKA

She felt the words fluttering in the room before he said them. With one hand she smoothed her hair. With the other she tried to quiet the beating of her heart. Even so she would have to prepare dinner, do the accounts. But the words were going from side to side, flying about (without lighting) like black butterflies, brushing her ears. She took out the kitchen notebook and a pencil. The pencil point was so sharp that when she wrote, it ripped the page. That hurt. The walls of the room narrowed around her and even the gray eye of the window seemed to observe her with ironic gaze. And Juan's coat, on a hanger, looked like a menacing phantom. Where could she find another pencil? In her purse there was one, smooth and warm. She wrote: gas, $18; milk, $2.50; bread, $1.25; squash, $.80. The pencil melted softly on the schoolpaper lines, almost like a balsam. What to give him for dinner? If there were at least a chicken. He liked it so. But no, she would open a can of deviled ham. For God's sake! She hoped the room wouldn't smell of gas.

Juan continued smoking, faceup on the bed. The smoke from his cigarette rose, losing itself in his blue-black hair.

"You know what, Manuela?"

Manuela knew. She knew there was still time.

"I know, I know. You had a good time on your vacation. But, what are vacations, Juan? They're no more than long Sundays, and Sundays make a man vile. Yes, yes, don't interrupt me. A man is nothing without the dignity his two hands and his daily obligations confer on him. . . . Haven't you noticed how clumsy men look on the beach, with their printed shirts, their mouths open, their sunburns, and the slow but sure bulging of their bellies." (My goodness, what am I saying! I'm on the wrong track!)

"Oh, Manuela," mused Juan, "oh, my English governess! Do you think they'll have beaches in heaven, Manuela? And big wheatfields that mix with the clouds."

Juan stretched, yawned again, folded his legs, curled up, and turned his face to the wall. Manuela closed the notebook and also turned her face toward the wall, where a shelf was covered with the objects she had bought herself with a great deal of effort. Like so many nervous unmarried women, Manuela had filled her desires with "marvelous things" absolutely necessary to her life. First a costly reproduction of Friar Diamond, opaline blue with little gold stars. "Friar Diamond, heavenly saint, if I don't have it I'll die!" The price was much higher than she had imagined. It meant overtime at the office, original and three copies, two new monographs, prologues for student books and doing without the theater, without butter, without the little glass of cognac before sleep. But finally she got him. After fifteen jubilant days in which Friar Diamond illuminated the whole room, Manuela felt her desires hadn't been satisfied. Then followed the music box with the first notes of Beethoven's Pastoral; the landscape supposedly by Velasco painted on a postcard with stamps and everything; the antique clock in the form of a locket that had probably belonged to a young Camelia-like and tubercular girl; the samovar from St. Petersburg like that in "The Dog's Lady" by Chekov. Manuela walked her virginity like a dry leaf by these objects.

Then one day Juan came with his hands soft like smooth leaves full of sap.

At first she didn't see him as any more than one of those students who listens eternally to the same jazz record, with a cigarette in his mouth, a lock of hair in his eyes. How can one love a lock of hair so much? As one who upsets teachers because he's full of difficulties and pure like the unicorn, so false in his protection of the maiden.

"Professor, could you explain this to me after class?"

The tiger came near, insinuating and perverse. Manuela firmly adjusted her eyeglasses. Yes, he was one of those who ends up scratching deep enough to take years to disappear. He glided around her. At every turn she was in danger of falling, because he crossed in front of her without looking at her but roaring incomprehensible things like those heard in the sky when it's going to rain.

And one day he licked her hand. From that moment, almost unconsciously, Manuela decided that Juan would be the next "marvelous thing" to take home. She'd put a collar on him and a chain. She'd lead him to her apartment and his soft body would brush her legs as she walked. There she'd place him on the shelf next to her other whims. Perhaps Juan would break them into bits, but what did it matter! The collection of "marvelous things" would come to its end with the tiger finally stuffed and mounted.

Before making an irrevokable decision, Manuela went to confession.

"Imagine, Father, I still have this mania of buying whatever object I feel like and this time I'd like a little tiger."

"A tiger? Well, that's all right. Tigers are also God's creatures. Take good care of him and return him to the zoo when he's big. Remember St. Francis."

"Yes, Father, but the problem is that this tiger has a man's face and tiger's eyes and a tiger's friskiness and all the rest a man's."

"Ah, that must be the species Felinantropus dangerously erectus. My dear daughter, in this school of letters and philosophy they teach the students strange things. . . . The advent of nominalism or the confusion of name with man has caused many young women to stray and overthrow traditional values. Don't think such silliness. As a penance you'll pray a rosary and three hundred three brief prayers."

"Hail Mary full of grace."

"Begotten without sin."

Manuela said the rosary and the prayers: "Striped tiger, pray for me! Eyes of burned sugar, pray for me! Eyeteeth of ivory, bite my soul! Canine teeth, ripe me apart in the name of pity! Pink palate, swallow me to the tomb! May the fires of hell consume me! Tiger, devourer of sheep, take me to the jungle! Crack my bones! Amen!"

The prayers over, Manuela returned to class. Juan smiled, showing her his sharpened teeth. That same afternoon, giving in, Manuela put a collar and chain on him and took him home.

"Manuela, what's for dinner?"

"What you like best, Juan. Mammees and raw fish, thick and elastic."

"Do you know what, Manuela? There at the beach I chased very green girls who turned pink in my arms. When I embraced them they felt like sponges, slow and absorbent. I also caught mermaids and took them to my bed and they turned into rivers all night long."

Juan disappeared every year at vacation time and Manuela knew that one of these escapades would be definitive. . . . When Juan kissed her for the first time, throwing down her glasses in the school hallway, Manuela told him "no," that people kissed only after a long friendship, after a constant and tenacious pursuit of words and plans. People always kissed with ulterior motives: to get married and have children and establish a future, not to comply with the will of the other. Manuela was weaving a long chain of commitments, of res-pon-si-bil-i-ties.

"Manuela, you're as awkward as a bird learning to fly. I hope you learn. If you go on like this, your words won't be bunches of grapes, but dried raisins of virtue. . . ."

"Kisses are roots, Juan."

On the stove, a fly lay immobile on a drop of syrup. A tender fly, sweet, heavy, and drunk. Manuela could kill it and the fly wouldn't know what hit it. That's how women in love are: like fat flies who give in because they're full of sugar.

But something unexpected happened. In her arms, Juan began to turn into a pussycat. A lazy housepet, a soft stuffed toy. And Manuela, whose ambition was to be devoured, now heard only quiet meowing.

What happens when a man stops being a tiger? He purrs for his domestic tamer. Impetuous leaps become timid jumps. He gets fat, and instead of confronting kings of the jungle, he dedicates himself to hunting mice. He's afraid to walk the tightrope. His roar of love that used to fill the silence with the sound of birds is now a sigh on the roof tile about to crumble.

Before the transformation, Manuela increased to 407 the number of her prayers: "Striped tiger, come at night! Tigerman, fill the storm! Dark stripes, turn to honey! Sacred veins, take me to the bottom of the mine! Cave of ferns, seaweed moisten my soul! Tiger, tiger, dive into my blood! Cover me with delicious wounds! King of heaven, unite us once and for all and kill us in a single soldering! Improbable virgin, let me die in the cusp of the wave!" If the prayers had any effect, Manuela didn't note it in her diary. She did write one day with a shaky hand—she wrote it surely without glasses—that her heart had slipped through a crack in the floor and she hoped someday to follow it.

Juan lit another cigarette. The smoke rose slowly, concentric like a holocaust.

"Manuela, I have something to tell you. There at the beach I met . . ."

There it was. The calm river overflowed and the words spilled out in torrents. They fell like excessively ripe fruits beginning to rot. Round fruits, intoxicating, primitive. Prelapsarian words that return us to the natural state: to sand, palm trees, and serpents, sheltered by the great green and gold tree of life.

And Manuela saw Juan among the foliage, reassuming his tiger role for another inexpert Eve.

Nevertheless, Manuela and Juan talked. They talked as they never had before and with the usual words. At the time of the rupture, floodgates open. (Hasn't it occurred to anyone to construct in their own life a runoff for excess?) Then the conversation ran into a hostile and insurmountable force. Human dialogue is a mysterious necessity. Above all the words and their meanings, above the pantomime of hand and face, there exists a law that escapes us. The time for communication is strictly limited; beyond it there is only desert and solitude and rock and silence.

"Manuela, do you know what I'd like for dinner?"

"What?"

(In the silence there were no more birds.)

"A little milk."

"Yes, kitty, that's fine."

(There was a scar in Manuela's voice, as if Juan had lacerated it hoarse. It would no longer reach those high notes of laughter. It would never unleash a scream. It was a bonfire of dead ashes.)

"Just a little."

"Yes, pussycat, I understand."

And Manuela had to admit her tiger was sick of raw meat. How that wrinkle in his brow was accentuated! Manuela wearily brought her hand to her face. She covered her mouth. Juan was a pussycat but hers forever. . . . How the room smelled of gas! Maybe Juan wouldn't even notice. . . . It wouldn't be so easy to turn it up a little before going to bed, when she went for the dish of milk. . . .

Translated by Elena Poniatowska

Go Figure

For Nancy Alonso

MIRTA
YÁÑEZ

I could watch everything Miss Betty did. Not out of any particular curiosity. Hardly. It was out of boredom, a boredom as huge as the Capitol Building. I've had my foot in a cast for almost two months, and I've still got a ways to go with it. So I don't leave my bay window, I might as well be chained to it, just like in the movie with James Stewart, that actor who always has to play the good guy. My grandmother used to say your face is a portrait of your soul. True enough, Miss Betty's face is like the face of a sparrow with a cat watching it, I'd say. Well, in the movie it's more or less the same thing. This James Stewart, with his kindly face, has his leg in a cast and amuses himself looking out the window. All of a sudden, boom, he realizes that something very strange is happening in the building across the way, one of those buildings with a lot of little windows and a fire escape. Where Miss Betty lives there's no fire escape because in the first place it's not in the Bronx or anywhere like that, it's in a tenement in Old Havana, you know. And in the second place because it's on the ground floor. But it's the same thing. What James Stewart discovers without moving from his armchair is nothing less than a murder and since the plot has to thicken, it doesn't occur to him to call the police or anything, or else he does call and they tell him to get lost, I don't remember which anymore. The main thing is that he starts doing some freelance detective work and begins to phone the other guy, the assassin, who has the kind of face you'd expect, emanating evil from time to time and all that, and finally the devil really gets into the bad guy and he's ready to tear James Stewart to bits, and the cops show up right then, which is always really stupid in mystery novels, but they get there just in time and of course, the happily-ever-after ending, everyone is pleased as punch except you know who, and then James Stewart with his good guy's face probably tells a joke, and the curtain falls with a final burst of laughter all around, like in those American movies that waver somewhere between Greek tragedy and the Three Stooges. Come to think of it, I'm not sure whether I should tell this story as a tragedy or a comedy. Miss Betty is about fifty thousand years old and leads a completely solitary life. Every evening, after she gets home from work, she makes herself a cup of tea without sugar, waters the plants, and then stands there with the watering can, looking out into space, for over half an hour. I swear it. Then she pulls a rocking chair up close to the door that opens onto the patio to take in the fresh air, the night dew. My grandmother said that it isn't good for you to breathe dew, but no-body'd better go and say that to Miss Betty. And anyway, I don't think she has anything else to do. She just stays there, rocking, until people start going out to work the night shift. Then she pulls in the rocking chair and turns out all the lights except the one in the entry hall. Day after day, the same operation. The truth is that she must feel lonely as hell. As far as I know, she's had three husbands. The first died of an embolism in a whorehouse, she herself tells the story, but Miss Betty would never dream of saying whore, so she says "women in the life," a phrase I've never understood very well, be-cause isn't everyone in life? I'll leave that problem alone. She lost the first husband that way, and the second one was run over by a train. Gentlemen, that's what you call bad luck. How many people do you know who've been run over by a train! I've only heard of Anna Karenina. And that was because she threw herself onto the tracks. But in Miss Betty's case, pow, a train comes and cuts her second husband in half, and he seems to have been a great guy, the one meant for her, and he was giving her industrial quantities of happi-ness, but that happened during capitalism and almost nobody in the neighborhood remembers it now. Although I imagine Miss Betty does, especially when she's out there in the dew. Right? The third one, the last chance, the lucky number, the triad, the three-cornered hat, the three musketeers, the three little pigs, the three Villalobos, the three Marias, good things come in threes, the Matamoros Trio, the three of hearts, the great one-two-three dance step that guy Hegel invented, the third time's a charm, brought the final catastrophe. The third little pig left on the Mariel boat lift, and that time the one who almost had a heart attack was Miss Betty. Because she's very revolutionary and does all the committee work. Imagine, she even picks up bottles to recycle for raw material and everything. Nobody ever expected Mario Rodríguez to leave her stranded, to her own devices, as they say. The guy never got involved in anything, but he didn't fool anyone. An opportunist, I tell you. When he did a plumbing job, a private one, I mean, he stuck it to his client, deep into center field, he nailed you, fifteen shots of rum just to change a washer, that really shows you what he was like. But Miss Betty, going from home to work, from work to home, she probably didn't know the half of it. And on top of it all she loved the guy. Those things happen. So she almost died of sadness. For three days she didn't leave the house, but one thing's for sure, Miss Betty doesn't want to hear of marrying again. Things that hurt, you have to pull out by the roots, even though a part of you goes with them. The bad part of it is that she's as lonely as a street dog, just like the words to that tango. That's why she's having all these problems. Miss Betty, well, of course she's no Miss, I mean her virginity, which she must have lost back in Machado's time, because otherwise she's very well-mannered and discreet. That's something my grandmother used to say: a discreet person doesn't butt in where they aren't wanted, just the opposite of what I'm doing now. They called her "Miss" because she's been a schoolteacher all her life, and the neighborhood kids always knew her by that name and it stuck. She isn't "Betty" out of any imperialist apocope, out of cultural penetration, or anything like that; what happened is that when she was born, in the time when jazz was young, they named her Bertilda, and that's too hard a name for kids, everyone must realize that, because, well, Miss Betty was really patriotic and respected traditions even before, when the bad guys were in power. That's why she almost died of embarrassment when Mario Rodríguez, the third little pig I told you about who was moreover her umpteenth husband, sold his toolbox and went to Yuma. Now, you know Yuma is street slang for the pesky North. I have no idea where that name came from, but it's pretty good, because first you let out the *YU* so it seems you're going to say it nicely and then you suddenly finish it off in that tasteless, cowboyesque way they have of speaking up there. So it's more graphic to say Mario Rodríguez left for Yuma, bringing the final A out of your wide-open mouth as you let all the air out of your lungs with a great big dose of scorn. As though you thought you were talking about a mouse. Although I guarantee you that some mice are better than people. But I'm getting off the point. Miss Betty doesn't talk about Mario Rodríguez that way, or about anyone, to her it was as if he had died. She never mentioned the guy again, or let even one silly little tear fall. Good for her, right? What I don't understand is why she's so bent on living alone, since she's still got plenty of fire in her. It's a real drag to live alone like that. And it's why all those things happen to her. The little kids climb up on her wooden fence and pull the planks loose, and it just stays like that. Her water tanks leak, and you can't expect her to crawl around and change the valves on them, so they keep on leaking. The breeze knocks her TV antenna out of place, and now she can't get Channel Two anymore. Until some neighbor's heart breaks in three pieces and he climbs up on the roof to fix it for her. You see, Miss Betty doesn't like to go around bothering people or asking for things. A tragedy, one hell of a hullabaloo. From my observation point I attended the opening: a cry as if she'd seen Boris Karloff in person, crockery flying through the air, broken glass, and a big hustle-bustle in Miss Betty's kitchen.

"What happened?" I asked her, and in passing I showed her my foot in its cast so she'd understand right away that I couldn't really help; she was defenseless in her enemy's claws.

"A mouse, a little mouse in the cupboard," she answered, and added for the sake of clarity, *"in my kitchen."*

This last thing she said like a trumpet announcing the last judgment. I opened my eyes wide and bit my lower lip in a simultaneous sign of surprise, nausea, and solidarity, a grimace that no words could have replaced. We Cubans are like that, half the time we'd rather gesticulate than converse. We must have gotten that from the Italians, through Columbus. All you have to do is see one of those Italian movies to tell whether we seem alike or not, especially the Sicilians. Listen to an argument in the house of a Cuban family and you won't deny we're just alike. I'm not kidding. This is an original theory of mine, but nobody has paid any attention to it yet. If you do, you're the first. Just imagine that scene, with Miss Betty holding on to her housedress as though it were going to split open from top to bottom, one foot bare and the other in a slipper. A hideous countenance. Complete desperation, you know how that is. With her hair so disheveled you could hardly imagine it, her eyes whirling out of their orbits, and her throat about to let loose another jungle yell, she could very well have been any shot of Anna Magnani, seconds before shouting *mamma mia!*, but Miss Betty couldn't say such a thing for two reasons, obvious ones, believe me. First and foremost, because she's got a very clear sense of the absurd, and second, because as far as I know, she doesn't speak Italian, even though she's read Dante's *Inferno* about eighteen times. So what she said was "Oh, my God!" five or six times in a row before closing the kitchen door. Speaking of hell: that isn't the end of it. Two minutes later she came back out into the hall armed to the teeth with a pile of newspapers and a broom. The newspapers really intrigued me, I won't pretend they didn't.

"The hunt has begun," she said sotto voce, and I raised my arms in a gesture that meant this: Courage, courage!

Miss Betty began to cover everything with the newspapers. Would the house catch on fire? The worst of that is that I would be the first victim. You know, because my foot's in a cast. Gentlemen, suddenly a light went on in my head: Miss Betty was covering all the conduits through which the undesirable entity might reestablish himself in her kitchen. With tremendous patience she took piles of paper and covered the drainpipes, the flues, the holes in the window, the nooks and crannies of the flowerboxes, the garbage can, the narrow space between the tanks of butane.

"It's got to get out of here this very day," said Miss Betty out loud, and I felt obligated to respond, considering that I was her only available audience for a million miles around.

"It's probably more than one. They have their young all over the place," I said, and realized immediately I'd stuck my foot in it. Miss Betty looked at me as though all the mice in the neighborhood were lodged in my person. Or at least as though I were their key accomplice. I displayed an idiotic smile to smooth over my blunder, but she wasn't looking at me anymore. She kept on bustling around with her newspapers. Well, what happened was I started to understand her strategy. It was to force the mouse to leave the cupboard, turn the corner very nicely into the hall I told you about, take the direction of the patio, and of its own accord get lost in a gutter *per secula seculorum*. She didn't want to have to draw blood like some Lady Macbeth. Well, what do you think of that! Bye, little mouse, there's no need for rancor, we can still be good friends. I almost died laughing at that. So I didn't miss a single move as she emptied the cupboard, pot by pot, can by can, bottle by bottle, rag by rag, and damn, there went that obstinate little mouse at the speed of sound, from corner to corner, crawling over here, climbing over there, confused in face of the mountains of newsprint. "How the countryside has changed!" it probably said to itself, running at the highest velocity, like a rocket, and Miss Betty jumping up and down with the broom in her hand, she looked like an Apache, I swear it on my mother's grave.

"Out, out, damn mouse!"

It was one hell of a chaotic scene.

The mouse, just like that, when it got tired of the little game, went straight to its private rooms in the cupboard. Well, this running back and forth I'm telling you about was just the beginning. The next Sunday she started the whole process over again, with the newsprint hills, the cardboard dikes, and the broom over her shoulder.

"You don't think the mouse has won?" I asked.

Miss Betty looked at me seriously, though she didn't seem mad or anything. I don't know how to explain it. It was as though she were under a spell , as my grandmother would have said. At it again, she emptied the cupboard, but in a more careful, better-planned way. The way she set things out this time, in the shape of the Great Wall of China, gave the intruder only one possibility: peaceful surrender. No violence. Who would have calculated that, splash! it would fall in the flowerpot with no dirt in it, full of water, a medieval moat, considering the tiny size of that mouse. Miss Betty marched along, holding the broom up like a lance, all ready to deliver the final blow. Then she saw the mouse's soaked and totally defenseless body. We can assume its frightened eyes were fixed on its executioner. Imagine the result: Miss Betty held out the broom, which from being a homicidal weapon turned into a life-saving ramp, and the shipwreck victim ran up it to take refuge once again in the cupboard, *her kitchen* cupboard.

"It would have been a crime to liquidate him like that," she said, and watched me with a mixture of shame and defiance.

"Of course," I answered with my usual stupid little smile. Numerical superiority. Sporting ethics. "Why don't you try a cat?"

Now Miss Betty's gaze made me feel like a professional torturer. "And how do I get rid of the cat afterward?" she murmured.

Operation Mousetrap began the next day. The first bait was a little piece of lunch meat that disappeared without producing a victim. Next she tried cheese, like in the cartoons. And the same thing happened. Finally she used a really appetizing piece of bread dipped in milk. Each time the trap was sprung and the mouse was just fine, thank you.

"A diet to gain weight," I said, and nobody laughed. "This mouse is a marvelous animal. He's outsmarting you."

"Put yourself in his place," she answered in an indecipherable tone.

"What?"

"Just that: a delicious lunch and then what awaits you? Death!"

"Chilling! When you put it that way, it seems really horrible."

"It is."

"And why don't you pardon him? He's earned it."

This time she answered angrily: "You're crazy. Typhus, bubonic plague. He's got to go somehow, it doesn't matter how."

But as time passed, I think she got used to the idea of sharing her kitchen with that mouse. She stopped chatting with me and started talking to herself: "Poison in the corners. No way. That's a disgusting system. Then he dies just anywhere and you don't even realize it. Only the stench clues you in. How disgusting!" Every day Miss Betty got more pensive, more melancholy. Thinner than a new shoot of sugar cane. That early morning when the sound of the mousetrap and the screeching of the mouse awakened half of humanity in Miss Betty's house, that is to say, the noise awakened Miss Betty, I was still in my watchtower, with a face like James Stewart and everything. The hunt seemed to have come to its end.

"I'd rather not face *that*," she exclaimed without addressing anyone in particular, but I've already told you, it was about three in the morning and I felt as though she and I, if you didn't count the mouse, were the only people awake on the planet Earth. I saw that she was opening the cupboard door slowly, and now her shout was a combination of horror and relief: "The tail!"

"What?" I shouted for my part.

"He lost his tail and managed to escape."

Miss Betty leaned out into the hall and then she did address me, with a lugubrious voice, like in a funeral parlor:

"His luck has started to run out."

I started to think the strangest thing, something like the things that hurt when you have to pull them out by the roots, and suddenly she said:

"By the roots."

Thought transference—you think?

It wasn't until much later that events accumulated and I found out what happened in the end. Miss Betty had gone to look for her can of tea in the cupboard. Absentmindedly she pulled open the door and without meaning to, she caught in it the mouse whose name we never knew. I want to tell you that he died instantaneously and with dignity. He left no heirs. I didn't see Miss Betty for about a million days. When she finally came out to water the plants, she stumbled all of a sudden on my gaze.

"He escaped from everything to end up dying by a fluke. Go figure," she said.

Miss Betty started sobbing, and she wept, wept, wept, as never before, I had never, nobody had ever seen her cry.

Translated by Leslie Bary

About the Authors

CARMEN BOULLOSA was born in Mexico City in 1954. She is a poet, novelist, and dramatist. Her novels have been translated into several languages. In 1989 she received the prestigious Premio Xavier Villaurrutia, and has also received grants from the Guggenheim Foundation and the Centro Mexicano de Escritores. She currently resides in Mexico City, and when she is not traveling, runs her own manual press which publishes art books.

ROSA MARIA BRITTON was born in Panama City in 1936. She lived in Cuba for several years, and studied medicine in Madrid, where she specialized in gynecology. She studied Oncology while residing in New York for twelve years. After returning to Panama in 1973, Britton spent more than ten years as director of the National Oncology Institute in Panama City. She has won the Ricardo Miró literary prize several times as a novelist, short story writer, and playwright. She currently resides in Panama City.

JULIETA CAMPOS was born in Cuba in 1932. She is a well-known fiction writer and has published over a dozen books, ranging from novels and short stories to critical literary studies. She has lived in Mexico since 1955, and currently resides in Mexico City.

ELENA CASTEDO was born in Spain and grew up in Chile. She has held dozens of jobs, among them teacher, translator, demonstrator of electrical appliances in shopping malls, model, and editor of a trilingual scholarly magazine. She has received a Woodrow Wilson Fellowship as well as fellowships from the American Association of University Women and Harvard University, where she received her Ph.D. Her first novel, *Paradise*, was nominated for the 1990 National Book Award. Ms. Castedo is married and has three children and seven grandchildren. She currently lives in Cambridge, Massachusetts.

MARTHA CERDA was born in 1945, in Guadalajara, Mexico. She founded and directs a writing school (la Escuela de Escritores SOGEM) in her native state of Jalisco. She is the author of four distinguished and award-winning books, and her short stories have been translated and included in anthologies worldwide.

DIAMELA ELTIT was born in Santiago de Chile in 1949. She has published four novels, one of which has been translated into English, and two into French. She has also authored a sociological study.

ROSARIO FERRÉ was born in Ponce, Puerto Rico, in 1942. She has published several volumes of fiction, poetry, and essays. She has also written children's stories and published literary criticism. Ms. Ferré currently resides in Washington, D.C.

MAGALI GARCÍA RAMIS was born in Santurce, Puerto Rico, in 1946. She is a journalist, essayist, and fiction writer. Her work has been published in Puerto Rico and the United States. In 1989 she received a Guggenheim Fellowship to work on her second novel. She has also been a lecturer and visiting writer at various universities. Ms. García Ramis currently resides in Puerto Rico.

ANGELA HERNÁNDEZ was born in 1954 in Jarabacoa, Dominican Republic. She holds a degree in chemical engineering, as well as being an essayist, poet, and fiction writer. She has published two books of poetry, several easays, and a collection of short stories, from which several pieces have been anthologized in Chile, the Dominican Republic, the United States, and Austria. Freedom, the limited nature of knowledge, and the destruction of innocence are recurrent themes in her work.

BARBARA JACOBS was born in Mexico City in 1947. Since 1970 she has been writing and publishing fiction and essays. She has been the recipient of various literary prizes such as the Xavier Villaurrutia (1987) and the National Fund for Culture and the Arts grant (1992). Her work has been translated into German, Italian, and English, and she has lectured at several universities throughout the U.S. and Latin America, including Berkeley, Stanford, New York, Iowa, Central Florida, Oviedo, and Buenos Aires. She currently resides in Chimalistac, a colonial residential area in southern Mexico City, with her husband, Augusto Monterroso.

VLADY KOCIANCICH was born in Buenos Aires in 1941. She has been a journalist, literary critic, and translator. Her novels have been published in Spain, Brazil, Germany, Great Britain, Italy, France, Norway, Sweden, and the United States. In 1988 she received the Premio Jorge Luis Borges given by the National Fund for the Arts, and in 1990 the Premio Gonzalo Torrente Ballester. She currently resides in Buenos Aires.

ALCINA LUBITCH DOMECQ was born in Guatemala in 1953. She has written over thirty short stories, and has published two books. She currently lives in Jerusalem.

ANGELES MASTRETTA was born in Puebla, Mexico, in 1949. She is a journalist and fiction writer, and a member of the editorial board of *Nexo* magazine. Her novel *Arárrancame la vida* (*Mexican Bolero*) was awarded the Premio Mazatlán in 1985. It has since become a national best-seller and has been translated into English, French, Italian, Dutch, Swedish, Turkish, Norwegian, Hebrew, Portuguese, and Finnish. Other works by her will be published in English by Plume in 1996.

CARMEN NARANJO was born in Costa Rica in 1930. She has served as Ambassador to Israel as well as Minister of Culture. Ms. Naranjo is an accomplished poet, novelist, and essayist. She has published over fifteen books and is recognized as an activist for women's causes.

CRISTINA PERI ROSSI was born in Montevideo, Uruguay, in 1941, and in 1972 sought exile in Spain, where she has resided ever since. As a poet and fiction writer, she has published nineteen books, which have been translated into nine languages. She was recently awarded a John Simon Guggenheim grant for her work.

ELENA PONIATOWSKA was born in Paris in 1933. As one of Mexico's leading literary figures, she is a novelist, essayist, and journalist. Several of her books have been translated into English, the most recent being her novel *Tinísima*, based on the life of photographer Tina Modotti.

MIRTA YÁÑEZ was born in Havana, Cuba, in 1947. She has published poetry, short story collections, a novel, and a book of criticism on Latin American romance novels. Three of her short stories have been translated and anthologized in the United States.

Selected Bibliography

RELATED ANTHOLOGIES

Correas de Zapata, Celia C. *The Magic and the Real: Short Stories by Latin American Women*. Houston, TX: Arte Publico Press, 1990.

Cortina, Lynn Ellen Rice, ed. *Spanish American Women Writers*. New York: Garland, 1983.

Erro-Peralta, Nora, and Caridad Silva-Nunez, eds. *Beyond the Border: A New Age in Latin American Women's Fiction*. San Francisco: Cleis Press, 1991.

Esteves, Carmen C., and Lizabeth Paravisini-Gebert, eds. *Green Cane and Juicy Flotsam: Short Stories by Caribbean Women*. New Brunswick, NJ: Rutgers University Press, 1991.

Manguel, Alberto, ed. *Other Fires: Short Fiction by Latin American Women*. Toronto: Lester and Orpen Dennys, 1986.

CONTRIBUTORS' WORKS IN TRANSLATION

Campos, Julieta. *Fear of Losing Eurydice*. Translated by Leland H. Chambers. Normal, IL: Dalkey Archive Press, 1993.

——. *She had Reddish Hair and Her Name Is Sabina*. Translated by Leland H. Chambers. Athens, GA: University of Georgia, 1993.

Castedo, Elena. *Paradise*. New York: Washington Square Press, 1990.

Ferré, Rosario. *Sweet Diamond Dust*. New York: Ballantine, 1988.

——. *The Youngest Doll*. Lincoln: University of Nebraska Press, 1991.

Jacobs, Barbara. *The Dead Leaves*. Translated by David Unger. San Francisco: Curbstone, 1992.

Kociancich, Vlady. *The Last Days of William Shakespeare*. Translated by Margaret Jull Costa. London: Heineman, 1990.

Mastretta, Angeles. *Mexican Bolero*. New York: Penguin, 1991.

Naranjo, Carmen. *There Was Never a Once Upon a Time*. Translated by Linda Britt. Pittsburgh, PA: Latin American Literary Review, 1989.

Peri Rossi, Cristina. *Evohe: Erotic Poems*. Translated by Diana D. Decker. Washington, D.C.: Azul Editions, 1994.

———. *A Forbidden Passion*. Translated by Mary Jane Treacy. Pittsburgh, PA: Cleis Press, 1993.

———. *Ship of Fools*. Translated by Psiche Hughes. London: Readers International, 1989.

———. *Dostoevsky's Last Night*. Translated by Laura Dail. New York: Picador, 1995.

Poniatowska, Elena. *Dear Diego*. Translated by Katherine Silver. New York: Pantheon Books, 1986.

———. *Massacre in Mexico*. Translated by Helen R. Lane. New York: Viking Press, 1975.

Acknowledgments

"So Disappear" by Carmen Boullosa was originally published in *Mejor desaparece*. Copyright © 1987 by Ediciones Océano. Rights reserved by the author. Translation copyright © 1995 by Heidi Neufeld Raine.

"Death Lies on the Cots" by Rosa Maria Britton was originally published as "La muerte está sobre los catres." Rights reserved by the author. Translation copyright © 1995 by Leland H. Chambers.

"Allegories" is reprinted from *The Fear of Losing Eurydice* by Julieta Campos, by permission of Dalkey Archive Press. Copyright © 1993 Dalkey Archive Press. Copyright © 1979 Julieta Campos. Translation copyright © 1993 by Leland H. Chambers.

"Ice Cream" by Elena Castedo is published by permission of the author. Copyright © 1995 by Elena Castedo. Rights reserved by the author.